WHAT KEEPS ME HERE

ALSO BY REBECCA BROWN

The Gifts of the Body

The Haunted House

The Children's Crusade

The Terrible Girls

Annie Oakley's Girl

WHAT KEEPS ME HERE

· ·

A BOOK OF STORIES BY

REBECCA BROWN

HarperCollins*Publishers*

"Someone Else" appeared in a slightly different form in *A Magazine* (Seattle: L.D. Publications, 1995).

"The Aqua Series" and "Bread" were originally published in *The Evolution of Darkness* (London: Brilliance Books, 1984).

"A Mark" was first published in *FRUIT* magazine (1995).

"A Severing" appeared in slightly different forms in *Rock Creek* and *The Bumbershoot Anthology,* 1985.

"What Keeps Me Here" was first published in *Active in Airtime* (UK, 1991).

HarperCollins books may be purchased for educational, business, or sales promotional use. For information please write: Special Markets Department, HarperCollins Publishers, Inc., 10 East 53rd Street, New York, NY 10022.

FIRST EDITION

Designed by Caitlin Daniels

Library of Congress Cataloging-in-Publication Data

Brown, Rebecca, 1956–
    What keeps me here : a book of stories / Rebecca Brown. — 1st ed.
      p.   cm.
    ISBN 0-06-017440-4
    1. Manners and customs—Fiction.   I. Title.
    PS3552.R6973W48   1996
    813'.54—dc20   96-12310

96 97 98 99 00 ❖/HC 10 9 8 7 6 5 4 3 2 1

Thanks to the MacDowell Colony for a residence in 1995. Thanks to Marlene Edmunds for the apartment in Amsterdam. Thanks again and always to Chris Galloway.

SOMEONE
ELSE

•••••••••••••••••••

••••••••••••••••••••••••••••••••••••

Someone else is in here. Not just me.

There isn't room for both of us, there isn't room for me. But she abides, inside, with me.

I think she's always been here, for she indicates she was. Though I have only recently admitted her.

When she is good, apparently, she's still and very quiet and except for the fact I know she's here, I almost wouldn't know.

But other times, and these times seem like all the time when I, when we, are in them, she is awful.

I don't know why she stays. She thinks I'm awful. Hates me. Loathes the ground whereon I walk, the very fact I do. I don't know why she lets me stay; she makes me.

Perhaps she wants to keep me here. Perhaps where I belong.

I have tried surrender. I have begged for my release: she will not answer.

Tell, I beg her. Tell. But she will not.

•

• • • • •

I don't know when I first discovered her. I say "discovered," but the more I learn the more I know that she has always been. Maybe she was waiting for a special time. She has a certain flair for the dramatic.

When I have tried to keep her under wraps and out of sight, she demonstrates. When I have tried to tell of her, she hides.

I have tried to go away. But there is no place I can go without her.

I have tried hard, I have tried very hard, to rid myself of her. I have tried to hold my breath, to pour the poison in, I tried it very hard, I do, I would. She always intervenes. I can't get rid of her—

Oh that's ridiculous. I could. I've read the books about the ways and they are numerous. The ordinary home, the common street, a grocery or a hardware store, they each have all the necessary means. A *child* could do it.

I wonder if I could have gotten rid of her. If, when I was a child, or first discovered her, I could have gotten rid. And if I could, could it have been without the loss, or rather, maybe less the loss that getting rid of means?

I tell myself, and I pretend and hope, she is preparing me. That she has come to ready me, to make me worthy.

I wonder is she merciful. I hope and pray, I tell myself she is.

•

THE AQUA
SERIES

● ● ● ● ● ● ● ● ● ● ● ● ● ● ● ● ● ● ●

• •

She likes the feel of the full fat slick round tubes, flattened at the end, and the hard ribbed knobs that twist off. She likes the slow pressure of her fingers squeezing the oil through the metal tip where it expands and eases as it hits air. She likes pressing oils on the palette, mixing them together with a blunt knife, swiping them thick on the canvas. She likes the softness of new brush bristles and the sturdiness of their solid wooden handles. Sometimes she applies paint directly with her fingers or the heel of her palm and feels the soft oily texture sticking to her hand. She likes the feel of pressing oil to the canvas, sometimes so thin she feels the crisscross grain of the stretched cloth on the other side of the film of color from her flesh.

She goes to the studio to work every day.

She wakes up in the morning at her apartment and opens the curtains to let in the light. She writes in her notebook, recording what she's done at the studio the day before and making notes on her plans for the day ahead. She doesn't take notes as she works. Every morning she checks the entry of the previous morning to see how she has put her plans into action. She writes things like:

•

Flame II: put more India/sienna in upper left. Corner offsets OK w/ yellow on lower rt. Also brown sphere now more sense of rising out of water.

Must do something else. Yellow/white highlight over sphere. (Will this be a "thing" planet?—) Thing-less-ness.

Muth's: 17 sienna. 3 navy.

After she finishes her journal notes she showers. She never showers before she sleeps. She always showers in the morning.

She goes to the bathroom and turns on the water so it will be hot and steamy by the time she steps in, then she brushes her teeth. Then she undoes her robe and hangs it on the door and steps into the shower.

Behind the shower curtain everything is steamy and hot. She takes the oval white soap from the soap dish and lathers her hands, rubs her stomach in circles and down her arms and legs in long lines. She rarely uses a washcloth because she doesn't like the coarseness of the cloth. She likes to feel the different textures of her body with her hands, and how the soap lathers hands, thighs, belly differently. She lathers up her whole body and has white beards of lather on her head and crotch. She usually keeps her eyes closed until she rinses, her eyes are very sensitive, but sometimes she opens them for an instant and sees her white, lathered head and white, lathered body in the cabinet mirror at the back of the shower. She can't see details but she can see the motion of her spreading soap over herself. She moves under the water, sticks her face up against the hot pellets and runs her hands against her skin as the

•

water splashes down. She rinses her hair, spreading her fingers wide and running them through. She feels soap rolls sliding down her neck and the points of her hair at the bottom of her neck. She opens her eyes and watches herself move her hands over breast and stomach, crotch and thighs. When she is rinsed, she stands up straight and lets the hot water come down hard directly on her face. Then she bends down and switches the faucets from hot to cold. There is a moment when the water slackens in the transition. Then cold water, made colder by contrast, beats down on her. She looks up again and everything blurs to yellow-red. Her eyes feel hot with shock, then cold. Then she turns the water off and hears the last drips from the faucet.

She pulls the shower curtain back and steps out of the tub into the bathroom. She pulls a large white beach towel off the rack and shakes her head, then rubs it hard. When she is dry she hangs up the towel, opens the door to the hall, and goes to her room. The air outside the bathroom makes her feel cold and clean, then warm. Then she puts on her clothes and goes to the studio.

She goes to the studio to work every day. She lives in a large apartment with an extra room she could use for a studio but she doesn't. She doesn't want her work and her life in the same place. Her studio is one large room and bathroom, with one large window. The studio is quiet, and though sometimes she hears the city outside, there is usually no sound except the swish and lick of her brushes and her feet across the floor.

At the studio every morning, she pulls the curtains open and lets in the morning light. Clear yellow light

•

washes over stacks of canvases, tables covered with paints, piles of newspapers, a bookshelf with all the books lined up straight, a storage closet, trash cans, easels.

Her work has been abstract for years. There always is the motif of light coming up through things that look like flesh or air, or snow or ice, through other types of light. Her basic method is this: She covers most of the canvas with a thin coat of yellow or gold, the "light." This coat is as anonymous as gesso. Then she layers on deliberately the colors that you look down through to see the light.

She works in the studio all day and when she comes home she doesn't think about work. She goes out some evenings but spends most of her time alone. Sometimes she falls asleep holding a book with the reading lamp still on.

But sometimes she turns out the lamp and looks. She sees colors and patterns and bending lines. She sees rows and rows of shiny blue dots and silver ribbons that sway like waves and deep blues that go under, further underneath. She sees opaque and liquid grays and jiggling cell-like circles. She sees a thin line of black around a white circle O, then a small black dot inside. Then she sees hundreds of them, quivering, a field of eyes. She sees a vast plane, empty, white, then—snap—a writhing jumble. She sees like a silent camera sweeping a giant arc over acres of texture, color, shape, of nothing.

Sometimes she presses her fingers to her closed eyes to see the sudden leap of red spread into orange, then pink. She rubs her eyes and watches blue and green. She puts her finger along the upper line of her socket and presses hard.

Her sleep is deep and she doesn't remember her dreams.

* * * * *

•

She conceived of *Aqua I* and *II* as a simple two-piece study of blue and greens over gold. It was to give the illusion of looking through layers of gauze toward a light. She expected to finish the piece in a few weeks, in plenty of time before an opening of her new work in her gallery.

But the *Aqua* piece didn't come off as planned. She didn't feel as if she'd finished the work with just two canvases, so she got another, larger one to turn into *Aqua III*. When she finished *Aqua III*, though, she still didn't feel finished, so she got a fourth canvas. Then she did a fifth. Then a sixth.

The day she finished *Aqua VI,* she lined up the six pieces side by side on her studio floor. She walked backward to the far wall, facing them as she moved. They looked like they were moving away from her. When her back touched the wall, she gasped. She was astonished at the amount of paint on the canvases and realized she must have used twice the amount on these six canvases as on any six canvases in the past.

When she looked at *The Aqua Series,* she didn't get the sense of satisfaction she usually got on reviewing a finished work. She looked at the individual pieces as if they were broken parts of things. She looked at the pieces in order from *I* to *VI.*

Aqua I resembled her earlier series—opaque thicknesses over a thin yellow base, like gauze in front of a light source. In *Aqua II* the gauze didn't float as easily and less light was let through. In *Aqua III* the gauze got heavier and covered two-thirds of the canvas. No light penetrated the cloth; it only escaped through spaces between. By *IV* the pale gold light was visible only in the tiniest slivers between dark pieces of cloth. By *V,* even these splinter-

•

thin exits for the light were obscured by layers of blue gauze. In *VI* the dark covered the entire frame; the underlying light was gone.

She stood in front of the *Aqua* series like a dog in front of a mirror. She stared as if she expected it to do something. She didn't know what she was looking at.

When she went home that night, she tried to read before she went to bed but she couldn't concentrate. She turned out the light and tried to sleep, but as soon as she closed her eyes and put her head on the pillow she saw the *Aqua* canvases rise.

They arranged themselves inside her eyes; she stared at each of them. She imagined touching the increasingly rough texture of each increasingly dark canvas. She imagined the roughness against her hands. She imagined walking around and looking at them from behind. She imagined touching the backs of them. She couldn't imagine what she felt.

The next morning when she sat down with her notebook to record what she'd done the day before she wrote haltingly:

Looked at Aqua.

She held her pen above the page, hesitated, then scribbled:

Finishing touches on Aqua. Must clarify statement of organic theme.

She'd never lied to her notebook before. She had no idea what *finishing touches* she meant. She had no idea what a *statement of organic theme* was.

•

She put down her notebook and took a shower. She turned on the water and brushed her teeth. She looked at herself in the mirror and saw the white foam circle forming around her lips as she brushed. She spat into the sink and rinsed her mouth. She undid her robe and hung it on the door and stepped into the shower.

She picked up the soap and was just about to lather when she decided to get a washcloth. She lathered her hands and scrubbed her body hard. She put her face directly against the water, then bent down to switch it from hot to cold. She opened her eyes for the second the water turned, and instead of the red-yellow splash she usually saw, she saw deep blue. Her skin felt cold.

When she got to the studio she stared at *Aqua*. She put the canvases in different orders, backward or starting from the middle. She spaced them evenly apart and at varying distances. She studied them from different angles of morning, afternoon, and evening light. She put them sideways and upside down. She stayed late at the studio again.

She went to bed soon after she got home. Before she slept, she saw *Aqua* again. This time the paintings wouldn't stay. They moved around against the insides of her eyes. They sat on corners and fell over one another and moved like they were being pulled by strings. They slid along in even planes like a magician's trick, the magnet beneath the table she'd seen as a child.

In the morning she bolted down her coffee and hurried through a scalding shower. The water was so hot it steamed the mirror at the back of the shower instantly; she didn't notice this. Though when she stepped out of the

•

shower, she felt cool. Her skin was a dark salmon color.

Her journal entry consisted of two words:

Aqua.
What.

When she got to the studio she arranged the paintings in sequence, upright with their backs to the window. Then she picked up *Aqua I* and laid it down on her worktable. She squatted down by the side of the table and put her eyes level with the canvas. She looked across the painting at the height of the paint. She remembered a relief map she'd done for a geography project in fourth grade. They'd built a huge box with a board base and four-inch-tall glass walls so you could see the layers of the earth, how the mountains and valleys had been formed. They'd made a crumbly paste of salt and water and flour, and they put it into bowls with food coloring: blue and yellow and brown and green and white, for water and sand and soil and plants and snow. She remembered packing the colored paste in the box and waiting for each layer to dry, to harden, before she put the next layer on top. She remembered the names, "sea level," "coastal plain," "piedmont," and how it had seemed forever until the word was for the white on top of the mountains: it was "snow."

She felt the texture of *Aqua I* with the tips of her fingers. The surface was sticky but firm. She pressed it. She brought her fingers to her face and smelled them.

She put *Aqua I* back in line and took *Aqua II* to the table. She examined the thickness of the paint; she touched it. She did this with the next four canvases. When she pressed her fingers to the surface of *Aqua VI,* it was moist,

•

it gave to her. She pressed her fingers in, then brought them to her face and looked at them. Her fingertips were dark. She ran her fingers down her face so she was painted.

When she went home that night, she picked up a book she had used in a restoration course. She read about matching colors to blend with the original and how to add highlights to the true colors. She read about paintings where one image had been painted on top of another and how sometimes the bottom image showed through.

There was a section on how to remove the upper image to reveal the earlier one beneath. She reread and reread this section. She thought about lifting the layers off. She closed the book and looked at the ceiling. It was flat and white and she could see everything there.

She rushed to the studio the next morning. The script in her notebook was almost illegible. Beneath her two previous entries—about *statement of organic theme* and *Aqua. What.*, she scribbled:

Uncover it.

When she opened the curtains in the studio, light fell over *The Aqua Series,* but she barely looked at them. She didn't pick up the paints or brushes. She picked up a palette knife. She laid the knives on the table according to size. She carried *Aqua VI* to the worktable. She laid it down and ran her hand over the surface. Her hand pulled across the colors and she felt the slip and wet of them. She wiped her hands against herself then braced the canvas on the table. She took a knife and began to scrape the thickest areas of paint.

•

She remembered when she was in grade school, coloring hard, pressing dark colors against the paper until she'd covered the whole page with thick wax, and then how she had scraped it off, scratching a pattern or her initials, a picture, but eventually an entire page, leaving only a pale memory of color. She remembered wax curls, like pencil shavings, on the floor, inside the creases in her clothes, between the pages of her coloring pad. She remembered the blue and purple and orange lines under her fingernails.

She leaned over the table and moved the knife back and forth. She felt muscles in her lower back and shoulders she wasn't used to using, the tendons in her wrists. Her body felt different. And the canvas looked different beneath her than it had upright, across from her.

By the end of the day she'd removed all the still-moist paint from *Aqua V* and *VI*.

She went home and read about removing paint. When she turned out the light, she pictured all six pieces in order, later, in the future, after she had stripped them clean. In her mind's eye she rolled off layers of darkness. Black, coffee brown, deep blue evaporated into green like pine and royal blue. The colors got lighter, like they were rising up through a pool. She watched them turn marine then sky blue, yellow-green, then finally clear. They rose.

She felt like she'd been rising too, from a cold blue lake. She'd felt the heavy pressure on her flesh and in her ears. Then she'd felt the pressure recede and she felt the sudden freeing break of surfacing.

She took two armloads of new supplies to the studio. She rearranged the room, setting the worktable, rather than an

•

16

easel, in front of the window. She packed the oils away into cabinets. She laid new palette knives across one end of the table. She picked up *Aqua IV* and continued scraping where she'd left off the day before. Sometimes the knife slipped and she cut herself and didn't stop to treat it. She leaned over the table and stretched. Her body felt different again.

She did this hard work carefully. But no matter how much she tried to do, she couldn't undo it all. The shadows of the colors stayed.

She remembered a room that was dark. There was only a red light above the door. She remembered seeing his hands and wrists, his hands were big and hers were small. She remembered seeing his chin move as he puffed on his cigarette without his hands. She was sitting on a stool, he'd lifted her up on it, her feet couldn't reach the floor. Everything was black or white or gray, or only lined with red from that small light. His shirt, her hands, the edge of the stool she gripped with her hands. His hands when he brought her down from the stool, his hands when he put them on her shoulders to guide her. He took her hand and they took the paper and slipped it in the water in the tray, she thought it was water. Her hand, with his, held the paper by its edge and swished it back and forth. He'd said to be careful and not to splash and told her to be patient and she'd see. Then she began to see: a smudge, a shadow, then that became more definite, and then a dark shape fixed itself. She saw a picture clearly through the water. Then he guided her hand to take the paper from the tray and the water dripped and he held it so she could see. It was a picture of herself she saw.

•

• • • • •

On the way to the studio the next day she bought two
long flat trays. She made up different mixtures of alcohol,
thinner, water, bleach, turpentine. She set the trays on the
table and poured in different strengths of solution. She
slipped a scraped canvas into one tray, swished it back and
forth, brushed the loosened paint away, then transferred it
to the second tray to soak. She watched the canvas soak all
day. It was late when she pulled the canvas from the tray.
The canvas was almost clear; only a hint of blue remained.
She hung it on the wall.

As the process of paint removal became more complex,
her notebook entries got longer and more technical. She
couldn't remember everything from one day to the next.
She began to bring her notebook to the studio and wrote
while the canvases soaked.

She looked over her notes when she got home at night.
One night she found this:

I don't know what I'm doing.

She didn't remember writing it.

One night she woke from a dream she couldn't remember.
She sat up in bed and turned on the bedside lamp. The
room was stuffy and she was sweating. For a second everything spun. She got up to go splash water on her face. On
the way out of the bedroom she turned on the overhead
light. She looked around the room as if she expected to see
something. She stepped back in. She looked inside the
closet. She checked under the bed and behind the dresser
and desk. She ran her hand under the bookshelves and on

•

top of the books. She felt through the drawers. She checked behind the wall hangings. She turned on the hall light on her way to the bathroom. She walked slowly, looking left and right. In the bathroom she splashed water on her face and as she was patting the towel to her face, she turned around and looked at the bathroom. She looked in the towel cabinet and behind the shower curtain. Then she walked through the rest of the house and turned on all the lights. She looked in every closet and cabinet, in the refrigerator and oven. She tapped the walls and looked beneath the rugs. It was completely quiet in her apartment and she sat down on the living room couch to listen. She didn't know if she had lost something or if it was something new. She sat on the couch the rest of the night with all the lights on.

She knew morning was coming by the pink that turned to bright light on her apartment walls. When it was morning, she stood under the water in the shower.

She took her sleeping bag and some extra clothes to the studio with her. When she got there she sat down and thought about the night. She wrote:

Spent half the night up looking around. All the lights on. What was I looking for?

She paused, then wrote:

What am I looking for?

Then she closed her notebook and started to work.

She watched herself go back through pieces she'd done three, four, five years ago. She started with old pieces that went back more years, before she had established her present style, pieces she'd done in art school and before. As she went through them, she noticed the increasingly repre-

•

sentational quality as she went farther back. She saw people and scenes and things.

These were much easier to strip because the paint was not nearly as thick or piled up as in her later work. She spent most of the day leaning over a surrealistic picture in which the forms of a woman and a man floated at an angle in the air on a beach by a mountain. The people were very small, their faces barely distinguishable. The colors weren't quite realistic; they looked like a color TV gone wrong, too flat and simple and bright.

She felt familiar with the picture, as if she'd seen it more recently than when she'd stacked it away years ago, but she couldn't place the association.

That night she worked late. She felt odd about her apartment and didn't want to go back to it. She spent the night in the studio.

She spent the next couple of days in the studio, going out only to pick up something at Muth's art-supply. The studio walls were covered with pale stripped canvases, pastel-colored from the tints that had worked into the fabric of the canvas itself and couldn't be removed. Drying canvases hung from the two lines she had rigged up on the ceiling, and a neat stack of tight rolled whitish canvas cylinders sat in a corner. Her stack of empty wooden frames grew accordingly, and she'd had to get two more garbage cans for the peeled-off paint. She had thrown the others out when they were full.

The second night she spent there, she watched the canvas darken to blue and gray until she could barely see their still forms in the dark. She lay on the floor in her sleeping bag and thought of the plain smooth surfaces around her on the walls. Everything was getting clear and light.

•

When she closed her eyes she felt safe. She saw the same white blankness in front of her eyes as she had on the white canvases. There was nothing there she couldn't see.

She went back to her apartment the next evening, and the feeling hit her again as soon as she opened the door. It was the kind of feeling that makes you stop and turn around and look over your shoulder for something, or just as you're leaving your house, makes you pause before you lock the door because you think you've forgotten something.

Except when she walked into the apartment, she knew that this feeling wouldn't go away. She went through the entire apartment. She went through all her books and looked under every piece of furniture. She took all the hangings off the walls and looked behind them and in between the glass and the picture. She started stacking things in piles. She moved all the furniture together to leave as big an area of empty space as possible.

In her bedroom, she emptied out all of her drawers. She felt underneath and behind them. She took everything off the walls and moved everything together and covered it with white sheets. She lay down, but she couldn't sleep. Even when her eyes were closed, she was looking.

She got up and turned on all the lights. Outside was dark, but everything inside looked white, the blank white walls, the blank white sheets.

She stayed awake the whole night. In the morning she walked into the bathroom and dropped her clothes on the floor. She stepped into the shower and turned on the cold water. It came out of the bottom faucet first, and she pushed the shower alternator and cold water came down

•

on her. She turned the water up full blast and stood in it, feeling the shock of cold on her. She felt points rise on her skin. She felt herself trembling and imagined her lips getting blue. Her skin felt hard and cold and prickly. She got the bar of soap and slipped it down her stomach, and it left a shiny slick track down her torso. She kept her eyes open.

Her body adjusted to the temperature. It wasn't comfortable but the shock wore off gradually. She saw herself in the mirror at the back of the shower. Her hip bones stuck out and her stomach curved in. She lathered her hair and felt her scalp tighten as if she were putting on a bathing cap. She put her cold fingers through her hair and massaged her head. She finished lathering and rinsed for a long time. She turned around underneath the hard steady stream of cold water. She stood still in one position, then moved and stood in another. She lifted her face up, directly into the shower, and opened her eyes and mouth. It hurt her eyes. They stung, but she kept them open several seconds and swallowed the cold water hitting her mouth. She didn't see anything.

When she finished she turned off the water and stepped out of the shower. She was freezing and she rubbed herself dry. She left the bathroom wrapped in a towel. Then she got dressed and got some clean clothes and towels and a coffeepot and hot plate and some cutlery and cups and plates and stacked them by the door. Then she turned off all the lights and took her things and left.

She sat at her worktable in the studio and opened her notebook. She looked at the blank white page then up at the canvases around her.

She didn't write anything.

•

She closed the book. She wanted to work but didn't know what to do.

She had stripped all the paintings. She thought about covering some new canvases with paint then stripping them, as if she could do a painting with the eventual strip-down in mind and be able to find what she'd been looking for. But she knew it wouldn't work that way. That would be like trying to test your own breathing rate, an unconscious action of your own, and the very act of observing changes the action.

She cleaned the place. She got rid of the worktables, her books and shelves. She let the easel go and all the paints. She threw out the frames from which she had removed the canvases. She threw out knives and brushes and trash cans full of peeled-off paint. She got rid of everything that could be hiding something.

When she'd cleaned the place out, she was left with four walls of shiny whitish canvases, each one faintly stained with color, and a floor made of the same. There was no place where anything could hide.

She sat on the floor and looked around.

She felt like she was finished.

There was nothing left to take away.

•

FAITH

· · · · · · · · · ·

Each of us is in a room and waiting. Each of us, both girl and room, is numbered. We have each been given numbers and we will be called accordingly. The call will be in order when the time is meet and right and each of us will stand upright and in the fullness of her time, and she will step, yes, when the time is meet, and stand—and then—

I don't know what happens next.

Although I know it will. The good thing will occur because it is the thing we're waiting for: the reason.

My number, that is, a number, whether mine or of the room in which I wait and consequently think of as my own, is written on the paper in my hand. (The hand I know is mine. Truly, wickedly, shamefully mine. For it has done the things—) The paper is small and thin and square. Though not, perhaps, exactly square. They aren't sticklers about the little things. It's the important things that are important to them.

The paper is smaller than my palm when flat. However the paper is rarely flat. For I have picked at it. I have held it to my mouth and nose to feel or smell, that is, somehow

•

27

discover it. But I swear, *I swear* I never tasted it. And I only did what I did because I wanted to know my number but the room is dark so I can't see so I had to touch it—

I rubbed it to my cheek and forehead, to my chest and neck, I curled it, rolled it thin, as skinny as I could, as any-one, well, any one of us girls—who knows what one of them could do, they could do anything, they know—I wish I knew—I wish—

I have curled it like a cylinder, a tube, of various sizes including: the size of a finger, the size of a cigarette, a size into which only a toothpick could fit, if that. I have curled it tight and made it stiff like a stick. Then I have tapped an end of it into the air, against the dark, the room I'm wait-ing in, as if this stick could penetrate—it can't—

I think I hear, almost, a voice. I tell myself to ready me. I pull my shoulders up and I am still and quiet like some-one wise, not like a girl. I almost hear, I think, I almost feel the air displaced by someone who's about to speak—

I have tapped the paper, rolled it against the chair, the hard and wooden arms, there are no cushions here but I do not complain, against the seat, the sides the front and back.

I have tapped the thing against myself. I have scratched it on my face and skin and I have stuck it in my ear. See, I am holding nothing back, I wouldn't hold the number back if I were one who knew it, I wouldn't put a soul through that.

Though it is true, I put—my hand has put the thing inside my mouth.

This action was done carefully. This thing was done so

•

it would not get wet and would not come in contact with the fluids and be dampened therefore damaged. I touched the paper again and again, in many ways, both hard and soft; I shaped it like a leaf, a stick, a tube, a fan that I then touched against the air, the floor, the parts of me, the parts of where I sat, in all the ways and places that I could. I did this in the hope my skin might feel a slight impression of the number that the pen or pencil, implement, machine had left imprinted. Or barring that, somehow, mysteriously, the way that psychics do with colors or with playing cards by touching, see.

But, no, I cannot truly say that I expected to discover the number by doing the former. Yes, I concede the former was ridiculous.

It could be said my care in doing these things indicates an ability on my part to distinguish between right and wrong, that is, to make a moral choice. But whether I could distinguish or not is beside the point because I couldn't help myself. And even if I could have—though I repeat: *I could not help myself*—I did these things in earnest, if not innocence, to learn my number.

I am afraid that something terrible has happened: The paper will no longer lie flat. I am afraid that I have picked at it so much that I have altered it. So now even if one could see, though no one can, it's always dark, and none of us poor girls can see, but if one could, say, one of them, one might no longer be able to see the number, but only see what a wreck I've made of the paper. It is no longer pure and clean as it was before I got to it. Before my grubby filthy horrible unclean hands—

•

But I was made the way I am. Surely they understand this. Surely, they can't blame me. After all, they made me and they are merciful and kind and they will pity me.

Three edges of the paper are straight, but the fourth has a nick as if the paper had been cut by hand, as if the person doing so had paused, midside, and readjusted the scissor. I wonder: Who did it? One of them? Or someone else, a minion? Was she interrupted? Tired? Did she nod? Was there some imperfection with the scissor? Did she sneeze? (Though I cannot imagine this.) What would have inter-rupted her? Would she have thought of me, my number? Would she consider not calling me—oh god—

This has not occurred to me before. It frightens me. But I must not be frightened. That would show a lack and I am faithful. I will get my call. As each and every one of us, yes, each and every one of us, as it is meet and right and in the fullness of her time, will get her call.

Both sides of the paper feel the same. That is, neither side has, say, the roughish texture erasable bond has on one side, nor the slickness that heat-sensitive paper has on one side either. I used to have one of those heat-sensitive type-writers in the mid-eighties. You could type without a rib-bon, just the heat would mark the paper, but you couldn't correct on that paper, and Wite-Out was a disaster. Only much later—it was too late, it's always too late—did I dis-cover what they didn't tell you when you bought those machines: The heat-sensitive paper didn't hold the type. It faded after several months like invisible ink. I discerned this when I found a bunch of my old papers and the words had faded and all I could see was smudges of what

•

had once been words and I couldn't read them. Or the numbers.

That paper and those machines were taken off the market a while back.

Good riddance.

Something just occurred to me: When I was saying I couldn't stop myself and they should know that I was made like that and pity me, I want to say here categorically that I did *not* do anything *so that* they would pity me. I didn't think about pity then.

Maybe they knew what I was doing but let me do it anyway. Maybe to teach me something. Maybe humility.

I hear, I think—

I tell myself it's time. I pull my shoulders up, and I am still like someone wise, not like a girl. I hear, I think— I feel the air displaced as if someone is just about to speak— about to call—

If they tell me I'm disgusting, foul and horrible, and filthy and I should have known, I will agree with them. I will apologize for everything, humiliate myself. And I will weep and hang my head and beg for pity.

Even if I did know my number, I wouldn't know how long I have to wait because I do not know what number they are on. Or if they're going through the numbers only once or more than once. Like at delis and bakeries, et cetera, where there's a machine and you take a number and read it, you can read it because it isn't dark, and estimate how long till you are called and if you should wait

•

or not. One thing about this deli machine: If there are, say, two hundred numbers in the machine, in a loop, after they get to 200 they start over again with 1, so conceivably you could be holding 198 or 199 but get called before 2 or 3.

There are so many possibilities. Even if I knew my number I wouldn't know enough.

Perhaps we do not know our number to insure that we will neither compete, nor covet, nor envy, nor bargain, trade or sell, nor steal someone else's. For if we know not our number, nor the number of another, we know not if our number is as bad, or better, worse, than hers. Hers could be worse. Poor fucker.

Perhaps we do not know our number in order to insure our constant vigilance. So that none of us could ever, say, if she knew her number was far off, get slack and snooze or misbehave or ask someone else to hold her place while she occupies herself with untoward, appalling, gross activities. Or just gives up when she finds out how much longer she has to wait because she can't fucking take any more—

Was it a crime to try to know? I can almost hear them telling me, though I have never heard them speak, to me or anyone I know, though, really, who do I know? Not a goddamned soul. But there are others here. There must be. I can't be the only one. Perhaps it was a crime.

I hear, I think—I tell myself Get Ready, and I pull my shoulders up and I am still and silent, almost like someone wise, not like a girl. I almost hear—I almost feel the air

•

against my skin displaced, as if someone is just about to call—

I open and close my eyes and see no difference in the dark. I used to wonder, though I now no longer do because it isn't right, it shows a lack, why one would get one's number on a paper if one cannot read because it's dark. Or, why does one get called aloud if one can't hear? For I think now one cannot hear in this place, it is sealed or soundproofed, something, so one does not, that is, I do not know if what I think I hear are sounds from someone or from something else or only just the gurgles swishes scratches of my noisy bloody horrible breathing body.

It is imperative they call me soon: *I cannot help myself.* Sometimes it's both: one palm open, paper thereon, the fingers of the other rolling it or—worse—folding it. Sometimes it's only one: the fingers on the paper in its palm. I do it all unconsciously, I do it before I know it, and by then it's already too late, it always is.

Because, I confess, as I already have, but I'll do it again, I've never lied at least, because I have rolled it into a little roll, folded it into a tiny square or rectangle or fan, not only will the paper no longer lie flat, it also is starting to feel furry like some arty homemade felt or cloth or rag, not like a paper you could write a number on.

I might as well fucking slit my own damned throat—

I wonder if I have been called already but didn't hear or recognize the call. Maybe I really can't hear, but maybe I really can. But maybe the things I think I hear are just inside

•

my ears, ringing caused by wax or moving horrible blood or flesh or air, or maybe they're only in my head, that filthy horrible place, or maybe when I think I hear the scratching, scraping, shuffling, is it in my room—or in the hall outside? For I assume there is a hall. Or if it's falling, being dragged? A cough, a slap, a cry—?

I think I hear—

My heart is beating very fast, my blood is throbbing and my stupid breath so loud— But someone else must hear and know that I am here, that I would answer if I could. I'm trying to—

I have to get a grip. I could get so excited I could have a heart attack. Or fall. Or drop the paper. Have to drag myself around and never find it.

I hear, I think, almost—I do? Almost—

I pull my shoulders up, and I get still like someone wise, not like a girl. I almost feel the air displaced as if someone is just about to speak, to call my number—I almost hear— almost—again—again—

•

BREAD

. . . .

For breakfast there were two kinds of rolls, white and wheat. We would get a basket of eight and there would be one, and sometimes—but only very rarely—two wheat ones; the rest were white. The white ones were long and looked like short croissants straightened out with four or five sections. We could see where they were wrapped around. They were white with thin butter glazing that made them yellow or gold or brown on top. They were in sections, and we could eat them in sections, tearing off a bite at a time and spreading a knot of butter on the soft open end we'd just pulled off. There was orange marmalade too, but I liked them more with only butter. The wheat ones were round around the top and sides but flat on the bottom. They didn't have glaze but were round and had specks of grain in them. They weren't as soft inside or in your mouth, or as sweet. We could just eat them; they weren't in sections and didn't have glazed caps to peel off or raisins to pick off. We could only tear them like a loaf of bread. They were small and fit in one cupped palm.

There was only one different way to eat them and there was only one person who did it that way.

•

It was you.

You never talked about it and no one ever talked about it in front of you, but everyone saw and no one dared do it like you. If someone else had started it, everyone would maybe have done it or felt they could have done it. Probably no one would have noticed it as something special if anyone else had done it.

But you had started it. It was yours and no one else's.

Someone would bring the basket to the table and put it in the middle. Everyone would reach for a roll, a white one, and when everyone had one, there'd be one left; you'd take it. It was always the last one, the wheat one. You'd lean forward in your chair and reach your right arm over the basket and flex your whole hand around it and pick it up and put it on your plate and put your napkin in your lap. Then someone could start the butter around and we could eat.

You would slice the one brown wheat roll through the side like a knife into a stomach. You'd cut the top from the bottom and sometimes the knife would catch and there would be a pileup of dough at the end where you split the top from the bottom.

You sat at the end of the table with your back toward the window that looked out into the yard. Sometimes I could see steam rising against the window from your just severed roll. I'd watch you put the two portions on your plate, bottom and top down, the exposed, soft insides up. You'd slice a triangle of butter from the yellow rectangle on the common plate and press it to your plate, then a tiny spoon of marmalade. Then you'd pick up the bottom half of the roll in your right hand and butter it with the knife

•

in your left. Then you'd put that half down, pick up the other, and spread marmalade on that. Then you'd put the knife down, pick up the bottom half in your left hand and put the two sides back together. Then you'd put it, assembled, back on your plate, wipe your hands on your napkin and pick it up and bite into it. Your teeth were straight and slightly yellow.

If there was ever more than one wheat roll, we'd argue over it because it was special, but also because they were better. If there were two wheat rolls, we'd all, all of us except you, rush to grab one of them. None of us ever dared touch both of them because one was reserved for you. Whoever got the second one smiled and was smug, and everyone else just took a white one.

We took turns bringing the rolls to the table. Sometimes people would volunteer out of turn to get them so they could touch the extra wheat roll, if there was one, and claim it before anyone else at the table had a chance. But you never had to do that. You never went to bring the rolls. When there was another wheat one whoever got it would eat it, tearing off pieces bit by bit, like a white one. No one could eat them the way you did. It was your way.

Our table didn't talk at breakfast. We were usually one of the first tables dismissed because we finished quickly because we didn't talk. You didn't like to talk in the morning; we didn't either. Sometimes you would look up from where you were sitting by the window at another table across the room if someone was talking loud or a group was too energetic.

•

Once you stared over at two girls telling a story to the rest of their table. One girl was thin and blond. Her fingers were like sticks and she kept snapping her skinny hands in the air to illustrate her story. She slapped the table and jumped around in her seat. Her friend was fat and very pale except for red cheeks. They interrupted each other, correcting each other and laughing. Their whole table was laughing with them. The fat one mimicked the accents of the people in the story. She puffed out her cheeks and lowered her fat double chin into her neck and spoke in a drawl. The skinny blonde screeched a narration. People at other tables were looking at them and trying to listen. We did too. The fat girl slapped her hands to her chest above her breasts and swayed her shoulders back and forth in a parody of her character's gestures. It was a good story and everyone was watching. I turned to the girl to my left to ask her for the butter, but I didn't ask because when I turned, I saw you.

You were sitting perfectly still, your forearms solid on the table in front of you on either side of your plate. You were staring at the two girls at the table. You hadn't eaten but one bite of your wheat roll. Your face was completely still. You were utterly silent.

I was ashamed.

I nudged the girl on my left. She was smiling at the story and she smiled at me, almost leaning over to say something. But when she saw my face she quit smiling. She opened her mouth to say something to me but I nodded at you. She looked at you, then dropped her head and snatched up her soft white roll, snapped off a section and stuffed it in her mouth. She kept looking at her plate. She ate another bite before she realized she hadn't put on the

•

butter or marmalade. She buttered the next piece, but the knife slipped and she dropped it on her plate. It crashed and she grabbed it with both hands. Her hands were shaking. We all glanced at her but everyone else turned back to the story.

I nudged the girl on my right and nodded at you. She looked at you and stopped listening to the story too. She nudged the girl at the other end of the table and kicked the girl opposite her under the table. We stopped paying attention to the story.

The story went on and on. I tried not to hear it. I tried to listen to the inside of my ears, the crinkly sound when everything is quiet, or just the sound of my chewing. I tried not to hear the girls, but I did.

Our whole table had stopped looking at them. Some of us stole sideways looks at you. You were still staring at them. It was a long, loud story. The fat girl was getting louder and the blonde was getting more animated. They had the attention of the whole room.

Then you did it.

The skinny one threw her hands in front of her to punctuate a point and knocked a cup of coffee on herself. She jumped up and screeched. Everyone at her table flinched and moved. Two girls on either side of her put napkins on her hands and arms where the burning coffee hit. They rushed her out of the room. Everyone else turned to their table and stared. People from different tables leapt up to get the Head Prefect and the Housemistress. Some other girls had gone to get the cleaning woman. Everyone looked up. Everyone flinched.

But you stayed still.

Our table still stayed still.

•

Then, when everyone was watching the aftermath of the accident, you began to eat again. You didn't say anything. You lifted your arms from the table, daubed your hands on the napkin in your lap and picked up your butter-marmalade wheat sandwich. You brought it to your mouth and bit.

At least one person from every other table went over to that table to ask what had happened and if everything was all right. But none of us did. We all tried to eat our rolls like you. We all looked at one another quickly. We looked at everyone at our table except you. You didn't look at anyone.

You willed the thing to happen. I knew. No one else knew, but I did. You knew I did.

We all felt ashamed.

I felt ashamed. I wanted to say, "I didn't mean, none of us meant—"

After the coffee was cleaned up things were quieter. You liked it more. You don't like conversation at breakfast, and you never liked it if someone else wanted it.

We all felt ashamed. We all wanted to be forgiven by you. You didn't look at any of us.

That girl got blisters on her hand. After that, we were all more careful.

You sat at the end of the table. The seating was arbitrary. No one was assigned. We just established ourselves in time. Technically, one would think the other end, opposite you, was the head because it was in the center of the room and closer to the head table where the Head Prefect or Housemistress sat, but the end you sat at was the head because you were there.

•

You sat at the head of the table in front of the window that overlooked the yard. I sat in the middle seat on the side of the table to your right. In the morning after breakfast the sun came in and lit you up from behind. Before someone put the lights on, and it was a little dark outside, your shadow went across the table a short way. When the lights came on, it disappeared.

One day there was a two-day period when there were no wheat rolls. You didn't eat white ones and we took the basket back at the end of breakfast with one white roll left in it. You didn't say anything about it. You just looked at the basket and didn't take a roll. No one else said anything about it in front of you. After breakfast, though, we talked among ourselves about it and made plans to go out and find wheat rolls for you if they didn't reappear soon.

We thought you were so strong to not even comment on their absence those two days. We talked about it for days, then long afterward. We admired your acceptance of the situation but reasoned that the position of being the one to eat the wheat roll every day went with the ability to deal with its absence. You had something we didn't have. You knew how to deal with things.

You were our heroine.

Every day they'd give us either buns for morning break or biscuits. Bun days were better. You wouldn't touch biscuits; neither would any of us. Buns had raisins and were soft. There was a thin layer of shiny glaze on top. They were soft and white around the sides but brown on the bottom from the tray and beige to brown to dark brown on the top, like shellac. When we tore them open they

•

were soft and white inside with raisins. We counted the raisins. We did it because one day you did it and the next day you suggested we all do it. We did it every bun day and started keeping tally, even when you weren't there. We reported to you when you came back. Sometimes someone would cheat. No one ever told you about cheating. It wasn't your business, but it was an issue between us. But I know you knew about it anyway. I bet you were pleased with it.

What was good was to take a small bite from the edge and break the surface and make an opening and then, poking and folding one finger into the warm inside, pull out a thick wad of pure soft bread. We made shells; we hollowed out the insides with a finger, and what was left was the shiny brown top and white sides and brown bottom and one hole in the side. Sometimes we found shells where someone had made one and left it.

We could also eat buns bit by bit, eating the top first, because often there was a thin pocket between the brown shellacked top and the white inside. If there was a bubble on the top, we could put a fingernail in and peel it off and either eat it in pieces or wait until the whole lid was peeled off, then eat them together. Then we could eat the soft part or give it to someone who liked that part if we didn't.

You taught us these ways. Even if you didn't think of each of them, whoever did presented it to you and you dismissed or accepted it. If you accepted it, you'd teach it to us. You never said whose idea it was if it wasn't yours, and in your presence no one ever said, "That's my idea." We didn't want to boast in front of you. But sometimes among ourselves, one of us would say, "That was my idea."

•

But we didn't listen to anyone else. You were the person who mattered. You were the person we loved.

Before every meal we had prayer. After everyone was in the room and at their table, the Head Girl or Housemistress would call on someone to say the prayer or say it herself.

The prayer was the same every meal. Only one person said it, and no one had to say it with her. The prayer was, "For what we are about to receive may the Lord make us truly thankful." Everyone said "Amen" and sat down or rushed up to the counter to bring back the food. If it was breakfast, one person from every table went up to get the rolls and then someone from the kitchen, sometimes the fat girl but usually her mother, wheeled out the cart with the pitchers of coffee. The coffee already had milk in it. They had it that way because without, it would make us nervous.

One morning I got there early and was washing my hands in the sink and the fat girl smiled at me. She was pouring the milk into a big pot of coffee. There was another pot of coffee without milk. I said, "Can I have some?" She smiled at me and I picked up the cup from the counter and scooped it into the hot steaming pot. The cups were glass. There was no pattern on them. They were old. The glass was thick and I couldn't see through it. It was rough from so many washings. I scooped it into the pot of black coffee. When I looked at the coffee through the cup, it was thin and brown. I tasted it and it burned my tongue. It was terrible. She poured bottles of milk into the pots. She broke the silver circle seals on the bottle lips. She punched her fat thumb into the center and broke open one side of the seal then she peeled it off and

•

scooped the cream off with a spoon and put it into a dish. Then she poured the white milk into the coffee in the big silver pots. I threw the terrible coffee into the sink and rinsed the cup and put it back on the counter. She picked up the cup and washed it with soap and water. She waited until the water from the faucet got steamy, then she got a dish mop from the tray and scoured the cup. Her fingers got pink. I thanked her for the coffee. Then I left the kitchen and went into the dining room and waited for breakfast.

We had prayer before every meal. The Head Girl or the Housemistress would say it herself or call on someone to say it. They could call on anyone. They did it that way to make sure everyone was paying attention to prayer. Some people didn't. Some people wouldn't listen or said it quickly to get through it. They rarely called our table, though. There was no need to. You were at our table.

It started this way.

One time she called on Philippa Rogers. Philippa Rogers did not believe. She skipped service each Sunday. The Head Girl said, "Rogers," and everyone bowed their heads. Philippa Rogers said the prayer. She said, "For what we are about to receive, may we all be truly thankful." We heard people pause for a second before we scooted our chairs to sit down or rush to the basket of rolls.

You didn't sit down. Everyone scooted their chairs and two people started from their tables to go get their baskets of rolls. You stayed standing. You didn't move. You said out loud, "That's not right." Everyone stopped. Everyone looked at you.

You stood at your seat. Your left hand was open and

•

your curved fingers were near the table and your finger-nails tapped the edge of the table. The fingers of your left hand stretched and tapped the table 1-2-3-4 like castanets. Your right hand pressed the table. The fingers of your left hand tapped the table: little finger, ring finger, middle finger, index finger. Your right had was clenched in a fist.

You only said it once. Everybody looked at you. Then everyone looked at their plates. You looked at Philippa Rogers. Your face was hard.

I heard you breathing.

You snapped your head back then lowered it. You closed your eyes and everyone looked at you.

Two girls at our table lowered their heads. Three girls at the table in front of us lowered their heads. Two girls at Philippa Rogers's table lowered their heads. When everyone's head was bowed, we heard a scrape as Philippa Rogers leaned too heavily on her chair, lifting two of its legs off the floor, and it fell back to the floor. I looked down at my hands. My head was lowered and I saw my hands clenching and my knuckles going white. I tried to see around me without moving my head. The girl to my right was clutching her napkin. I closed my eyes and didn't see anything.

Philippa Rogers cleared her throat and said, "For what we—" Then we heard her swallow. We heard the noise her throat made when the saliva went down from her mouth. She exhaled quickly through her nose, then said, like she was out of breath, "For what—for what we are about to receive, may the Lord make us truly thankful."

No one moved.

Then we heard you slide your chair out. We raised our heads. Your chair scraped across the floor and you sat

●

down and scooted yourself in. You put your forearms on the table, on either side of your plate. You looked at the girl at our table whose turn it was to get the rolls. You smiled at her.

She jumped up quickly to get the rolls. We all sat down. When the rolls came we ate them quickly. During the meal someone at Philippa Rogers's table dropped a plate. You didn't look up. You ate your wheat marmalade roll.

You were beautiful.

On Sundays we were required to go to church. We could go to whichever church we wanted to, but we had to go somewhere. The Housemistress or Head Pre would ask us where we'd been to make sure we'd gone. Also they would make spot checks at churches. They'd go to a different church every week to make sure people were where they said they were going to be. Christ Church was only two blocks away, and St. Philip's was three. There was also St. James and Parish Church and all the denominations. People went to different ones to keep from being bored. We could go to the early service at 7:30 and be back for breakfast or go to the later service after breakfast at 10:30. Everyone went to the later service because Sunday break-fast was at 8:45, fifteen minutes later than the rest of the week and we liked to sleep in.

On Saturday nights everyone would ask everyone else which church they were going to and make plans. Sometimes we took turns and four of us would sign out as though we were going to a church but then only two of us would go and the other two would do something else like shopping or going to Devil's Chimney or the Sandwich Bar, and if the Head Pre or Housemistress came

•

to that church and asked where the other two were, the two in church would vouch for them and say they were sitting behind the pillar or in the bathroom. No one went to church by themselves.

Except you. You went to both services every Sunday. You went to St. Gregory's 7:30 service every Sunday by yourself. St. Gregory's was far away, and you had to take a cab. Every Sunday morning at 7:00 a black cab pulled up by the front door of our house and you were waiting for it. You stood inside the tall bay window to the left of the door. You held the heavy beige curtain back with your left hand, and your right hand held your shoulder purse. Your fingernails shone. You did your nails the night before.

The cab drove into the driveway and stopped, but you were out in the driveway before he was even at the door and you'd wait for the cab driver to open the door for you and you'd get in. As you slid into the backseat, you tucked your coat beneath your hips. You wore shiny black shoes with wide high heels. You never wore them any other time except to St. Gregory's on Sunday.

One time I woke up early to go to the bathroom, and when I stood over the sink by the window washing my hands I looked out and saw you get into the cab.

Every Sunday after that I saw you from the bathroom window. I leaned on the white sink by the window to watch you. My feet were cold on the concrete. You wore your Sunday shoes. You never saw me.

Monday to Friday from 8:00 to 4:45 we wore our uniforms, and from 8:00 to noon on Saturdays. At 4:45 class was over, and we could change in the hour before we had to be back in the library to study or we could wait until

•

right before dinner at 7:30, but we couldn't be in our uniform at dinner. If shoes were too high-heeled or not polished, we couldn't wear them. In the morning on the way into prayers the Pres stood at the door into the auditorium and looked at our shoes. They made sure they were polished. If they weren't polished, we were dismissed from prayers and docked an hour of free time or had to report to the Head Divinity Mistress for extra divinity lessons. We got the Ones and Twos to polish our shoes. They liked doing it for us, and they'd compete for who got to do whose shoes. They tried to get the Pres' first, and everyone competed for the Head Girl. She awarded her shoes to different Ones and Twos to give more of them a chance. She always had her shoes done the best because she had all of them compete for her. Her shoes were the best of anyone's.

Except yours.

You did your shoes yourself. At first the Ones and Twos competed for your shoes like they did for the Head Girl's, but then they stopped. No one else in our form did her own shoes. We were too old, and the Ones and Twos wanted to do them for us. But you did. You did your shoes yourself. You did your shoes better than anyone.

To leave, we had to have it planned in advance and have our parents come or write permission and say where we were going. We had one weekend a month, plus half-term and Saturdays and Sundays. You were away more than anyone. No one else went as much as you. Your father came and got you every Saturday at 1:00. The first week of every month you spent the weekend at home. Every weekend after that you spent the day with him on

•

Saturday and came back in the evening. On Sunday you went to church in the morning and sat in your room for the rest of the day. In the evening after supper you came out and talked with us. You spoke with everyone the same.

One time you came back with a huge white box. Your father left it in the calling room when he dropped you off. It was Saturday evening. The box was huge. The Head Pre called a house meeting. You opened the box, and there was a huge Black Forest cake in it. It was at least three feet by two feet big. I'd never seen a Black Forest cake so big. I'd never seen a Black Forest cake half as big. It was gorgeous. Around the edge of the box on the inside I could see a rim of brown where the oil and cream had stained the white cardboard. There was dark brown and regular brown frosting. There were six rows of cherries. Someone from the kitchen brought a knife. You cut the cake. You asked someone from the kitchen for some napkins. She brought them. I was standing near you. She handed me the napkins. I put them on the table by the box. You picked up a piece of cake. I picked up a napkin. I handed the cake and napkin to the girl in front of me.

We did this for the whole house, thirty-six pieces of cake, plus two for the mistresses and three for the kitchen. We saved some pieces for people in the morning. You and I ate after everyone had their piece. The cake was good. The frosting was thick and smooth and creamy. The inside was brown sponge soaked with cherry liquid. Everything was moist and sweet and heavy. None of us had ever tasted anything so wonderful. All of us felt wonderful. No one asked you what it was for or where it came from.

We remembered that day forever. The next day we told all the other houses about it. Some people from

•

other houses said things to you, like they'd heard about it and wished they had been there, but no one asked you about it.

We talked about it forever. Someone said your father owned a bakery. Most people disputed this: Your father was too much of a gentleman. We didn't know why the cake had come.

Then the rumor started that it was your birthday. No one asked you and no one thought to ask the House-mistress. We didn't ask about your mysteries.

I started the rumor.

On Sundays I woke up early, every Sunday except the first Sunday of the month. I watched you from the bathroom window. I watched you with your shoulder purse. I thought of your shiny black shoes and your high black heels, getting into the cab on the way to St. Greg's. My feet were chilly on the cold concrete. Then I went back to bed.

In the morning they rang a bell half an hour before breakfast. I tried to be up earlier than the bell. I put on my robe and went to the bathroom. My robe was long and fake-velvet dark blue. It was soft and in a minute warm over me. I never put on slippers. If I was early there was hardly anyone else in the bathroom. In the bathroom were four toilet stalls and five sinks with mirrors over them and windows between them. Next door was a room with four little rooms with bathtubs. I went to the bathroom and washed my face and brushed my teeth. By the time I was finishing more people would be coming in and I would nod good morning if my mouth was full of toothpaste or say hello, and sometimes I wouldn't know who I was say-

•

ing hello to if my eyes were closed under soap. People were sleepy-looking and in their robes. Some people didn't talk at all because they'd just woken up and some people were in talkative moods.

When I finished in the bathroom, I went back to my room and got dressed. I undid my robe and it fell to the floor and I was naked. My uniform was hanging over the back of my chair by my desk. If it was cold I'd jump around and try to make my blood go faster with my hands and inhale through my teeth, a "ssss" sound, and wring my hands. I put my shirt on first. It was white and long-sleeved and I buttoned it all the way up, even the sleeves. It was straight around the bottom with no tail. I pulled on my underpants. They were uniform too. Then I put on my skirt, thin if warm, thick if cold. It zipped up the side and was plain. Then I put on my tie. I stretched the tie in my arms over my head then put it behind my head on my shoulders. Then I dropped it and pulled my hair out from underneath it. I tied the tie. The tie was green with red stripes going down it diagonally. It was the house tie and had a scarf to go with it too, red and green. It was very ugly. If it was too cold it took my hands a long time to tie it. Then I put on my sweater. I almost always wore the thick one, not the thin one, because if it was warm I didn't wear one at all. I pulled it over my head. When it was on I pulled my hair out from the sweater and straightened my tie and reached my hand up under my skirt to pull the shirt down and straighten it. Then I sat on the bed and picked up the socks on the chair and put them on. They were thick and soft and wonderful dark green. I liked them. I bunched them up over my hand and made a tight ball of my fist and put my foot into the little open-

•

ing at the end of my palm. My feet were freezing, even more than my hands, and sometimes I'd just hold on to my foot with my hand to try to make it warm. I put my foot in the sock and pulled the sock over my foot, then stretched it up my calf to my knee, smoothing and straightening on the way up then I put on my shoes. They were brown and plain and low. They were our uniform shoes.

Then the bell was ringing and I went downstairs for breakfast.

For breakfast there were two kinds of rolls, white and wheat. There was butter and orange marmalade and pots of coffee. There was a box on the shelf on the wall by the door and everyone grabbed their napkin from the box and took it to the table. After the meal was over we put them back. Everyone had their own box, their own napkin. They were white and stiff and rolled into a cylinder and stuffed in tiny boxes. We got them washed once a week with the laundry. By the end of the week the box was full of wilted, dirty napkins. There was only one napkin that was never wilted or dirty.

It was yours. Yours was always perfect.

On the first Sundays of the month when you were with your father you weren't there to eat the wheat roll in the basket. On those Sundays we'd rush to be the one to get the basket of rolls. We looked forward to seeing if we could get the wheat roll.

We talked a lot on those Sundays. We talked about you and wondered where you were and what you were doing. Then we just talked about where we were going to

•

church and what everyone was doing. We were often very rowdy the first Sunday of the month.

The Night of the Cake we got to stay up half an hour later. The Housemistress smiled and said she realized we were all too keyed up to get to bed at the regular time, so she'd let us stay up until eleven, providing she didn't see too many tired faces in the morning, and if someone wanted to go to sleep before eleven, no one was to stop them. We finished eating our cake way before then but we were all so thrilled we couldn't sleep or study. We just stood in the calling room talking. When the House-mistress said we had to leave we went to our rooms and talked. We talked until 11:00, and then, even after she had called lights out and did her rounds, some people snuck into their friends' rooms and stayed up late talking. The next day everyone was in a particularly good mood, though some in fake good moods because they were tired but had to fake it for the Housemistress.

I went to bed at 11:00 and stayed in my room.

I lay in my bed with the lights out and looked outside. I saw the orange light of the street lamp through the dots of rainwater on the window. There was steam on the window from the cold outside. The leaves looked orange and bronze in the light of the street lamp and sent out shoots of orange into the air. I heard traffic going by and people walking and laughing quietly.

I thought about holding the napkins you put your cake on and everyone else eating theirs before we did. In my mind, I pretended we were doing it again. I wanted to tell someone, but someone different, not the people going to each other's rooms. I stayed in my room and looked at the

•

bronze-leaved trees and listened to the traffic and people walking until I couldn't hear them anymore. Then there was no noise coming in from the outside. I closed my eyes and fell asleep.

Sometimes I saw you in the bathroom before breakfast. You were always completely dressed. You never left your room without being completely dressed. You came to the bathroom completely dressed and washed your face and brushed your teeth in full uniform. Your shoes were always polished.

You were always perfect.

I was in love with you.

When they were taking people for a special scholarship, you were one of them. It meant you went away lots to be interviewed and look at schools. It meant you missed breakfast because you'd leave after lunch one day and come back the next day for lunch or supper. Your space was empty at the table. Your wheat roll just sat there. We were afraid there could be a mistake and you might just come in late and what would you do if you didn't have your wheat roll? We were very careful.

One time Fiona Donovan asked me if I would ask you something for her. Fiona Donovan had been raised poorly. She had no social sense. She wanted me to ask you if you would help her with her Applied Mathematics prep because she had been out for a week. Everyone knew you were the best at Applied Mathematics. I told Fiona Donovan she was a fool. I said you had better things to do with your time than help someone with their problems

•

when she could get anyone to help her and what were teachers for anyway? Then she said, well couldn't I just ask you and I said, "Why me?" and she said, "You're the one who helped the Night of the Cake." I said, "Sure, but that's nothing." She said, "Everyone knows she told you it was her birthday the Night of the Cake." I looked at Fiona Donovan. I didn't say anything. I had made it up. You hadn't told me anything. I said to Fiona Donovan, "Yeah, well, so what? It's no big thing if it's your birthday. Why shouldn't she tell me?" I said it as nonchalantly as I could. I was thrilled. Fiona said, "Well, she doesn't say things like that to anyone. You must be her friend." I said, "Well . . ." I tried to sound secretive and humble. I didn't look at Fiona. I was proud. Fiona said, "Well, couldn't you just ask her—" I snapped my face up at her and said, "Don't be ridiculous. She doesn't spend her time with just anyone, you know." Then I walked away.

I pretended you had told me it was your birthday. I imagined you said my name. We were standing by the table holding our pieces of cake in our hands. You had cut a piece of cake and put it on the napkin I held. You said my name, and then you said, "Today is my birthday." I listened to you and looked at you and you were beautiful and it was your birthday.

For breakfast one person from each table went up after prayer to the counter and picked up a basket of rolls for the table. The person getting the rolls would put the bowl and plate into the basket and carry them back and put them on the table and take the bowl and plate out of the basket and put them on the table. We all got our rolls and passed the butter and marmalade around.

•

● ● ● ● ●

One day—it was a Monday after you'd been to St. Greg's—you weren't at breakfast. You were out some- where looking at a school or being interviewed for a scholarship. We knew you wouldn't be there and your place was empty. I looked at your empty chair and the wheat roll sitting in the basket. We all ate our breakfast and at the end I took the basket back to the counter and the fat girl who poured coffee with her mother saw me and smiled. She saw the wheat roll and looked at me. I said not everyone was at our table. She looked at the wheat roll again. She shrugged her shoulders and picked up the wheat roll then picked up the basket and turned to put the basket away. As she turned, I saw her pop the wheat roll into her mouth. She did it like it was nothing. My mouth fell open in awe. I stared at her.

The next day at breakfast you didn't come again. Someone brought the rolls to the table and there was one wheat roll and you weren't there. Everyone helped them- selves to a roll. I was the last one. There was one white one left and the wheat one. I reached for my roll. Then I paused, hand in air over the basket. I didn't turn my head, but I tried to look at everyone else. The butter was going around and people were eating. We didn't wait for every- one because you weren't there. I decided. I withdrew my hand and started again.

I leaned forward in my chair and reached my arm over the basket and flexed my hand around the wheat roll and picked it up and put it on my plate. I put my napkin in my lap and someone passed me the butter.

I sliced the wheat roll through one side, cut the top from the bottom and put the two portions on my plate,

●

bottom and top down, insides up. I sliced a triangle of butter from the yellow rectangle on the common plate and pressed it onto my plate, then a tiny spoon of marmalade. I picked up the bottom half of the roll and buttered it with the knife. I put that half down, picked up the other, and spread marmalade on it. Then I put the knife down and put the two sides back together. I put it, assembled, back on my plate, and wiped my hands on my napkin. Then I picked it up with both my hands and bit.

I felt the tiny crunch as my teeth broke the surface and went into the soft inside. I tasted the warm brown taste and the knotty texture of the grains and specks of wheat. The texture was tougher than the plain white rolls. It didn't taste as sweet in my mouth, but did taste more full. I could feel the slick texture of the butter and the sweet one of the marmalade between the layers of bread. The marmalade was almost gritty it was so thick. The white rolls were bland compared to this. I was happy.

Then you were there. You stood directly opposite me. I saw you and stopped chewing. My mouth was full of roll but it felt dry like I was going to throw up. You stared at me for a second then passed on to your seat. You moved so gracefully, like your feet didn't touch the ground.

Everything in my mouth felt full. I felt like I had already thrown up and it was in my mouth. I looked around at everyone else. Some people were staring at me but most people were staring at their rolls or plates and wouldn't look at me. The girl to my right made a gesture to pass the basket of rolls to you. There was only one roll in the basket, a white one. I was eating the wheat one, your wheat one. You didn't shake your head, but almost.

•

She took her hand back and put it into her lap. She didn't pass the rolls to you.

My mouth tasted like vomit. I swallowed. The roll sat on my plate with one bite taken out of it. I looked at my plate, then closed my eyes. Then I looked up at you. You drank your coffee and looked at nothing. Then you smiled.

You were so kind and forgiving.

Then you looked away and drank your coffee in silence, not looking at anyone.

I tried to drink my coffee, but I couldn't. I didn't try to eat the roll.

I took the basket back at the end of breakfast. The one white roll was left.

The next day at breakfast, after prayer, you touched the girl to your right whose turn it was to get the rolls. You didn't say anything. You didn't need to. She sat down. Everyone else did too. I wanted to say, "No," but I couldn't.

You went to get the rolls.

All of us were silent. You'd never been to get the rolls before.

You brought the rolls to the table. You took the plate and bowl and put them on the table. You stood at the corner of the table, two people away from me, the corner closest to the counter on the opposite side of the table from your seat. When you'd taken the plate and bowl out of the basket, you didn't put the basket on the table.

Here's what you did.

You offered the basket to the girl on your left, my right, and she took a white roll. Then you offered the basket to the girl on your right, and she took a white roll. You

•

moved around the table and offered everyone a roll and everyone took a white one.

You'd started with the girl on my right. I was going to be the last one.

When you came to me, I reached up to take the last white one, but you pulled the basket back. I said, "What are you doing?" You didn't answer. You reached your right hand over the white roll as if to take it out of the basket and put it on my plate, but you didn't. You took the white one out and held it in your hand. Then you turned the basket over on my plate. The wheat roll fell on its side then fell upright.

"What are you doing?" I whispered.

You put the empty basket down in the center of the table. You sat down. You turned to the girl on your left and held out your hand. She passed you the butter. You had a white roll on your plate. It looked deformed in front of you. You had never eaten a white roll before.

I looked at the white roll and felt spit in my mouth.

I couldn't eat. My stomach felt hot like there was a bubble in it. My mouth was full of water.

The butter was going around and everyone was buttering their plates and their white rolls. When the butter came to me, it stopped.

I looked at you and said, "What are you doing to me?" I said, "Why are you doing this to me?" You didn't look at me. You tore off sections of your white croissant roll. Everyone else looked at their plate or roll.

I looked at the girl across from me. I said, "What is she doing?"

She didn't look at me. She only looked at her white roll.

•

I looked at everyone. Everyone was eating white rolls. You were eating a white roll. No one looked at me. Nobody would look at me.

I sat there and I couldn't move. I closed my eyes.

Inside I saw the color of your St. Greg's Sunday shoes.

•

THE PRINCESS AND THE PEA

There's something in the bed, she says.

In the middle of my loving her she stops me. Our damp familiar bodies part. We're in our bed in her family home which she inherited. This room was her girlhood room. We have lain together here for years. She takes my hand in hers and whispers, No. Her voice is frightened. I put on the light. She's sitting up, her head is lowered, her shoulders hunched. She looks like a frightened child.

She's naked as we always are in bed, but shivering. I tuck the sheet around her and I put my arms around her and she trembles.

I feel something in the bed, she whispers.

I don't know who she doesn't want to hear. There is a shiver in her body and I hold her then we leave the bed and she sits in the chair. I pull the blanket off the bed and wrap it around her shoulders. I shake the top sheet of the bed, I run my hand along the bottom sheet, I shake the pillows out and there is nothing.

I can't see anything, I say.

She sits in the chair with her knees drawn up, her chin

•

tucked in toward her knees. She looks like she is trying to disappear.

I go to her and sit on the floor beside her. When I look up her eyes are closed, her mouth is tight. What is it?

I don't know.

The next night I wake up alone. I reach across to her side and it's empty. Honey? I say. She makes a sound from across the room. It sounds like a little animal. I turn on the light beside the bed. She's sitting in the chair. She's wrapped her robe around her and her arms are tight. Honey, what are you doing?

I couldn't sleep.

I feel her side of the bed again. It's cold, she's been awake awhile.

But you're just sitting in the dark. She nods.

Honey, I say, Princess, what's going on?

There's something in the bed.

The sheets are rumpled, our pillows are punched the way each of us does, the mattress is pressed with the shapes of us.

What is it, I ask again.

Again she tells me, I don't know.

The next night when we've turned off the light, she pulls my body close to hers, she puts her arms around me tight and tells me, Hold me, Hold me, and I try. My face is pressed against her neck. I can feel and smell her skin. I breathe in deep and put my mouth against her skin; it tastes of salt. She clutches me tighter, her breathing skips. I move my head to look at her face and she tries to turn away. Her eyes are closed. I see the tears she's trying to

•

contain. What's wrong? Have I done something wrong?

It isn't you. She twists away from me.

What is it?

She shakes her head.

The next night she stays up late to work and I'm in bed alone. I try to stay awake for her, but after a while I can't. I turn out the light and try to sleep, but I hear her pacing in the study. She turns the radio on and off and rustles and tears up papers. She mumbles and catches her breath. But she's said she wants to be alone, so I don't go to her. Finally, when I fall asleep, I dream of her.

I wake in the dark and she's in the bed and I reach out to touch her but it's not her skin, she's covered. She's wearing a T-shirt. My hand is on her stomach and she puts her hand on top of mine so I won't move.

She says, and she says it low as if there's someone else she doesn't want to hear, Be careful.

So my hands are careful on her shirt, and kind and slow. The cloth is soft between our skin. I run my hands down the back of her shirt, then slip my hand beneath the hem until she tells me, No.

I remove my hand and she clings to me like something could tear her away; I try to hold her. I hear her trying not to cry. After a while she takes my arms away from her and lies down on her stomach. I put my hand on her back but she shakes her head and mumbles, No.

She lies on the edge of her side of bed. We lie like that, not touching in the dark.

The next night she is covered more. She's wearing sweatpants and a shirt. When I get into bed she pulls me close

•

and holds me and we don't say anything and then she's crying.

She tells me something is pressing her. She says she feels like it's behind her, creeping up on her, but also like something that's already done. She asks if I will look at it. She sits up, turns her back to me and lifts her T-shirt. I move into the light to look. I see the beautiful skin of her back, the bumps of her spine, the ridges of ribs, the muscles of her shoulders. I see her tan lines and the freckles on her milky, milky skin. But I do not see any marks.

Here? she asks, and twists her hand around to point. I don't see anything.

Maybe here? She points to another place. She sounds tentative, as if she's frightened and hopeful at once.

I'm sorry, I say, but I can't see any marks.

She lowers her shirt and turns around to face me. Do you think I'm just imagining it?

I believe you, I say.

I don't know if I believe myself. What if I'm imagining it?

There's something here, I say. I don't know if she wants me to believe her.

She wants me not to touch her anymore. She cries when I lie next to her, then cries that she is pushing me away. I tell her it's okay, I understand, that we'll find it and get rid of it then everything will be the way it was. We do the things we think might help. We wash the sheets and blankets more, and we get new ones: cotton, flannel, silk. We get hand-embroidered pillowcases from the ladies at the church, and feather pillows. We check the mattress for loose buttons, springs. We take out what's beneath the bed, our suitcases and winter clothes, the boxes of her photographs. We get a different

●

mattress, box spring, futon. We get mosquito netting, a canopy. But nothing works; she feels something in the bed.

One day when she goes out I strip the bed and take the mattress and box spring off and I undo the slats and frame. I'm going to rebuild the bed so there isn't room for anything to slip or creak or pinch.

She comes home in the middle of this and says, What are you doing?

I'm going to reseal everything, put it back together more solid. I gesture at the mess on the floor and try to sound lively, like this is just a question about furniture. It could be something really small, I say, like a splinter or a knot in the wood. It could be something the size of a pea.

Don't—

I'll put it back together—

That isn't it. I know you will. Just don't.

Why not?

It isn't yours. She takes a breath, it's hard for her to say this: It's mine. Whatever it is. I have to find it.

She looks at me. It isn't in the bed.

I nod as if I understand, but I don't.

She clears her throat and says quietly, It's in me. Then she drops her head in her hands and sobs.

I step toward her to hold her, but she tells me, Please don't touch me, and I back away.

She looks at me, her face is red. You're trying so hard, she says.

Yes, I say, I want to find this thing too. I don't want anything to hurt you.

I know. But I need to find it alone. This isn't something someone else can help me with.

•

Suddenly I'm very frightened. Sweat springs all over my body.

Then she enunciates very clearly, she's been rehearsing how to say it. She says, I have to change this relationship now. She draws up her shoulders and says, I need to sleep alone for a while now.

That's okay, I understand. I say it quickly without thinking because I don't want to make things hard for her. But as soon as I say it I'm angry because it's not okay and I don't understand, I don't understand at all.

Then she says, I know this will sound odd, since I'm the one who feels something in the bed, but would you mind letting me sleep there and you sleep on the couch in the study?

I'm so startled I say, I don't mind. I say this without thinking too.

Thank you, she says. She sounds miserable. I think she starts to say something else, but she leaves the bedroom.

I watch her back retreat. Her shoulders are trembling. She's crying. But I know not to touch her now.

I look at the disassembled bed. As I reinsert the slats I look at every one. I examine every seam and joint and every crease and corner. I run my hands along each surface where a splinter could arise. I put my ear to every creak. I check the bed for anything we might have overlooked. I want it not to be a thing inside her.

In the mornings I see her at breakfast. I try to talk with her. I ask her how she slept. She doesn't tell me. At first she's pleasant and polite, but there's a brittleness to her. It isn't just her body she is pulling back from me.

● ● ● ● ●

●

One desperate day I try to act like there is nothing wrong. I say, Hey, Princess, let's get a new bed. We can rearrange rooms, put the new bed in the study and turn the bedroom into the study and—

That won't help, she says. It's the first complete sentence she's spoken in ages.

I don't say anything.

It's not the bed, she says, It's not the room—

What is it? I reach out to touch her arm and I see her flinch. She clutches her arms in front of her chest. There is terror in her eyes.

What is it, What is it, I ask again.

But she can't tell me.

That night, as usual, I go to the study to sleep on the couch. But I don't sleep. I lie in the dark and think of her. I think of how often in the past she wouldn't ask if she needed or wanted help. Things as simple as, I'm working at home, and she's gone out to run errands for herself, and when she gets back with a car full of packages to bring in, she won't ask me to help carry them in. Or we're making dinner, I'm doing salad and beans and she's barbecuing salmon steaks and one falls in the fire and burns and she insists that it was hers, that I eat the other one and she won't let me give her half of it. I think how both of us are like this, we rarely ask for what we need because we don't want to impose, because we don't know what we need. I think how rare, in some ways how good, it is that she asked me to leave the bed because she asked me for something she needed. We've cut ourselves off from one another by not asking. I think of the times I wanted her help but didn't ask her. I think how part of me wanted her to just

•

know and come help without my asking. Then I tell myself she must be like this too. I tell myself that, though she hasn't asked me to be in there with her, she wants me there. That is, I convince myself that she wants me to go to her.

So I get up and go down the hall, I stand outside the closed door of our bedroom and I put my ear against it and I listen. At first I can't hear anything. But I want to hear so much, I strain, I hold my breath, and then I do hear something. I hear her breathing unevenly, I hear her turning restlessly in bed. I hear the whisper of the sheets, the puff of the falling blankets. But then I wonder if I am imagining, if I could be hearing things because I expect to hear them from what I think I remember. I wonder if there is something else that I can't hear at all. I put my hand on the doorknob and I turn it slowly until it clicks and I open the door and go in the room and shut the door behind me.

The room is dark, the curtains are closed. The room is still and the air feels dense the way it does before a storm. I look at the bed and see the shape of her body. The covers are bunched around her, she's lying on her side. I start to step toward the bed when suddenly I can't move. Something is hard against my chest, it's pressing me, it holds me back. I open my mouth to cry out loud, but I can't make a sound. It feels like a hand.

Then I see something stirring in the bed. The sheets are pulled away and she's uncovered. She gasps, she tries to pull her body in, she puts her fist against her mouth to keep from crying out. There is the pressure of something on the bed. My heart is beating, terrified. I try to shout, to stop the thing except I can't. There is the pressing in the

•

bed, I hear the muffled cries, the pleas, then there's a hand, a mouth, against the mouth, there is the sob, the gasp for breath, the creak of something moving in the bed. She tries to go inside herself, she tries to fold up far inside where nothing else can get. She tries to fly above herself, above the awful bed. Then I see in the dark above the bed, as far away as she can get, a shape. It's like a vapor, a hologram. It is a shape, inside of her where nothing else can get. It stays above the awful bed and sees the hiding self. I know that I can't stop it, I cannot undo what's done. But in my mind I cry to her, I tell her that I see.

After this night of the awful sight she can no longer bear to stay where it occurred. So in the morning when it's nearing light, she says she needs to find a place where what has been remembered can become forgot again. She says she has to go alone, and be with no one else who knows, or who has seen or witnessed what was done. That is, she tells me tearfully, she has to leave me.

I don't want her to leave, I want to stay with her. But this time when I tell her that I understand, I do.

Now every day I pray for her. Every day, although I know that we cannot forget, and we cannot undo what has been done, I pray that she has found a place where she can live without the fear of the terrible thing that happened.

And sometimes I pray not only for her, I also pray for me. I pray there is another place where what has been remembered will no longer tear apart.

This happened once upon a time, a long, long time ago, before we had learned what had happened to us.

•

A MARK

. . . .

· ·

She came to me and told me she was marked. She said what they had done and this determined who she was. She said she did the things because of it: It soiled her.

She had to tell and asked me would I listen. I said, Yes.

She waited till the night was dark and there was no one else around because there hadn't ever been.

She took me to the room and said, Get in the bed. I did. She did it too. She turned out the light. The room was dim but I could see a little in the light that came in from the street. It made the edge of everything look bronze.

She lay on her back and I lay next to her. We did not touch but I could feel the warmth between the edges where our bodies didn't touch. I felt the cool of sheets against my hands and forearms, through my shirt.

I looked at her and saw a rim of wet around her eyelids but it didn't fall.

She sighed like she was waiting, then she sat up in the bed and I could see the profile of her face and then her neck and body through her shirt. She held the bottom of her shirt and lifted her arms and pulled her shirt off over her head. The air around us moved and I could smell her skin.

·

She breathed in deeply and her shoulders rose. The bronze line moved across her skin like water.

Then she turned her back to me and told me, Look.

Her back was wide and white or grayish in the light. I saw the square of her shoulders, her upper arms, the taper of her waist.

She asked me, Can you see it?

I squinted. I thought I saw something except it could have been a shadow or it could have not been anything. I reached to touch it, but she flinched and shouted, No!

I pulled away my hand. She did not turn around to face me when she spoke. Her voice was quiet and she said how it had gotten there. She said the things they did and they were horrible. I heard then saw how it had grown, how inward was the mark.

I saw, I could discern it as she told. The soiled place was in her skin, a brand. It didn't shine but it was dull. The mark was on the left but near the center of her back. It was above the middle and it lay across her ribs and barely touched her spine. The mark was almost oval, thinner at the bottom; wider, rounder at the top. It looked about six inches wide across the middle and eight or maybe nine inches high. It was about the size of a hand.

I listened to her tell and weep. Her arms and shoulders rose and fell with sobbing. She kept her back to me to hide her face.

She told me she'd attempted to remove it. She had tried it more than once, the same ways over and over again, and many other ways she wished she could forget. But she could not get rid of it.

Then she said it couldn't be removed by her alone, she needed help. She asked me would I do it, I said Yes.

•

Then she asked, You'll do it then you'll stay with me?

A second time I told her, Yes. I didn't want to lose her or abandon her.

Then she told me, Close your eyes, and so I did and she turned on the light. I felt the light across my skin, the room was different, things were seen.

I heard her breathe and wait until she could, and then she spoke, her voice was shaking, Look.

I opened my eyes and gasped. The mark was horrible, a hole, but full and dark and huge. Around the mark, and this was worse to me perhaps because I hadn't seen a hint of it before, there was a ring of scars, of thick white gnarled ropes. There was another ring of red and black and knotted scabs from where she'd tried to cut it from her flesh.

Inside the ring the mark itself was still intact, immovable.

She told me, Put your hand on it.

I wanted and I did not want to touch it but I did.

I opened flat my palm and lay it on the mark. I felt the ridges of the tissue with my fingertips, the smoothness of the scars, the crack and roughness of the skin. She leaned her back against me, and I felt her weight and then the muscle and the bone beneath the flesh. A hand fit perfectly. She took a breath, her body shifted. Take it away, she said, and I withdrew my hand.

Not that, she said, the mark.

I didn't understand. She turned her body partly around. She had a knife.

It's got to be cut out but I can't reach it.

She handed me the knife.

I couldn't speak. I shook my head. She pressed the knife against my palm. Her hand was hard but trembling.

•

You said you'd help me: *Help me.*

I can't do what you're asking with a knife. There has to be another way—

There's not, she cried.

I'm sorry, I said, I can't— I dropped the knife.

She cried out. Leave, she said, I don't want you to stay now with what you've seen.

She kept her back toward me so I couldn't see her face. No, I said.

I know you want to, she said. Leave. Then she was sobbing.

I got up from my side of the bed and went around to hers. She sat on the edge, her face was in her hands, she wouldn't look at me. I put my hands on her shoulders. She flinched a second but then was still. I put my hands beneath her elbows and lifted. Her body was surprised but she did not resist. She stumbled up and stood. I lay my hands on the sides of her face. I felt the wetness on her cheeks. I put one hand beneath her chin and lifted her face. Her eyes were closed. Her face was red and wet. She turned away, and I let go my hands.

Then slowly, when I hadn't left, she turned her face to me. She opened her eyes and we saw the other. I took her hands and lifted them. Her arms were limp at first and they did not resist. I pulled her arms around my back and she did not remove them. I put my arms around her back. Beneath my hands I felt the scars, the mark, I shuddered but I did not leave, and I did not remove my hands. I held her.

We stood unmoving for a time.

Then when she could, her arms around me tightened, she embraced me.

●

A SEVERING

· · · · · · · · · · · · · · · · · · · ·

• •

When you throw a clay pot, you slap it down on the wheel and center it. You firm it to the wheel by pressing it down hard on the edges. As you press the wheel you scrape the skin off the sides of your palms. Once it's centered, you shape the pot. You can do anything with it. Your hands press and squeeze it into shape and when you're through you remove it.

Here's how you remove it: You take a strong wire about three feet long. You hold the ends of it in each hand and wrap most of it around your hands for grip. You have to be careful or else you might cut yourself or cut off the circulation or leave lots of pressed white marks on your skin from the pressure. You get the wire tight around your hands and then you stretch the wire taut so it's about a foot between your arms. Then you stand on one side of the pot and put your arms over the other side like you're going to give it a nice big hug and you lower the wire to where the pot is just on the edge of the wheel. You press the wire into the clay where you want to separate the pot from the wheel and you pull. You pull the wire toward you and separate the pot from the wheel. The clay tears

•

apart under the pot as you scrape the wire along the concrete wheel. If you're an amateur, you'll probably mess the pot up around the bottom and you'll have to work at putting the smoothness and shape back into the bottom of the pot. If you're a pro, though, you can remove the clay from the wheel without doing much damage and people won't be able to see the marks.

I never got the hang of taking the pots off, myself. I'd always get a pileup of stuff on the bottom and then when I'd try to mend it, I'd make the pot a mess. Then I decided that if the pots I made wouldn't come off the wheel easily, I should let them stay on. A thing can get formed to another and trying to tear them apart can only be bad. I decided some things were meant to stay, and pots were some of them.

Most people don't think the way I do about pots. Some people are real experts at taking pots off the wheel. They take them off so easily you can barely see the evidence. They're so clever they can mend the bottom of the pot in no time. A quick rub and it looks like nothing ever happened.

I've become quite a pro too, in my own small way. For obvious reasons I quit throwing pots. But I developed a keen eye for seeing the kind of things people did, had done, would do about removing pots. I got so I could spot the marks, any marks. No matter how hard people worked at repairing, that is, disguising, the damage they had done, I could see it.

I started having fantasies that I was some kind of pot myself. Well, that's stretching a point. I'm only like a pot in one sense: I fantasize that there is this wire going through my head, slicing off the top of my scalp. And I

•

feel like a blob of clay, completely unable to act against it. I feel the taut slick wire being placed around my scalp. I roll my eyes upward to see the wire being eased into place. My eyes are rolled up and my head is tilted back like a mystic. I can see the wire being eased into place, but I can't see who's putting me in it. But I feel it tighten and my scalp begins to tighten like I'm putting on a bathing cap at the pool at Girl Scout camp when I was a kid in Texas, except I'm not a kid and this isn't camp, it's now. It can happen any time or any where: in my room, or on a street, or in my bed at night. The wire begins to tighten and I can feel my hair getting all pressed in and I'm thankful I have thick hair because it makes a cushion for a second or so, but then it can't anymore. Then I close my eyes and I feel the pressure build up around my skin and my head gets hot and there's red inside my eyes and pressure like being held under water too long and I can't breathe. The water's hot, it's about to burst, then all of a sudden the pressure breaks and it's hysterical. Like at the movies when there's really tense music and it gets dark and you know what's going to happen and then they cut off the sound and you can only see the silhouette of the friendly girl at the shop, she's thrashing around and you know she's screaming bloody hell but you can't hear anything because the sound is off.

That's what it's like when the wire puts that first blood squirt on my scalp. My eyes are clenched closed and I open my mouth to scream, but nothing comes out. I'm just there with my mouth dropped open but nothing comes out. This lasts a long time, I don't know how long.

Then after a long time, I don't know how long, it changes and I can feel something else. I feel warmth com-

•

ing down my head, a Benedictine wreath of blood drip-
ping down in a perfect circle. Then I can also feel a thinner motion upward as blood spreads up my hair like little
capillaries. Then I feel the crunch of my skull. Then I hear
it and I feel the splinters, slivers of bone against each
other. Then I'm shaking but I am trying not to scream
because I do not want to move but I have to. My whole
body is tight and clenched and then, when I can't stand it
anymore, I do, and all of a sudden something gives.

That's when the soft meaty part of my brain gets it. It
offers little resistance, like cutting a very soft and tender
marshmallow with a razor. The only resistance is caused
by bits of bone and hair that are wrapped around the wire.
I hear the sounds of squishing together. I open my eyes
and all I can see is red, like a curtain in front of my eyes.
Or solid clots of hair or bone slide over my eyes like an
eyelash. But pretty soon the soft ooze is mixed around and
I can't see or think and all I am is vaguely aware of the
taste, in my mouth, of blood.

Then there's one last jolt as the wire pulls tight, a little
bump where both sides meet. There's one last stab at the
back of my head, then the masterful tug as it yanks itself
from between the severed upper portion and the portion
still connected to my neck.

Sometimes there's a problem because my hair catches
on the wire and the top starts getting dragged off, but
somehow it always manages to get back in place. I actually
lose very little. It's rather that things are rearranged.

After it's over, I'm just there, dumb. Then, after a while,
my feeling comes back, I throb and I get sick from the
smell of blood. There's blood in my nose and ears and
eyes. I taste blood every time I swallow, and every time I

•

try to move I have to be very cautious because I'm afraid I'll lose the top part. And my clothes, of course, are absolutely ruined.

The blood in my ears feels like water in my ears when I was a kid after swimming, and my first urge is to stand on one foot and lean over and jump up and down the way my mom used to tell me to, but I'm afraid that if I do I'll lose the top part so I just wait awhile then try to get it out with Q-tips.

Then every time, as if I didn't know, as if it hasn't happened before, it takes me time to realize what has happened. Sometimes it takes me so much by surprise that I reach up because I feel like there's a bump on my head. Imagine my surprise when I touch my hand to my head and my fingers go in! The texture is warm and soft and moist, which is nice, but it hurts like hell. The salt from the sweat on my hands only makes it worse. I jerk my fingers away and bring them to my face and I see blood all over my hands.

After I've finally come fully around and see the shape I'm in, I am embarrassed. I try to clean myself up. It requires only the simplest things. I wash with soap and water and let it dry. Then I dab with alcohol. The alcohol stings but I know I have to do it for my own good. After that I put on some Vaseline. Then I wrap a long gauze bandage around myself and tie it tight enough to stay, but never so tight my skin can't breathe and never so tight it hurts. There is a balance. Then after I'm cleaned and bandaged I try to cover up so no one will see what's happened. It's really embarrassing.

I used to wear a bandana, but then they became so stupid, so lately I wear hats. I have a couple of cowboy hats,

•

WHAT KEEPS ME HERE

a straw one for summer and a black felt one for winter. But they draw attention where I live now (I no longer live in Texas), and I don't want to draw attention. So, tired as I am of the baseball-cap thing (I hate these stupid fashions), I do that. I don't know what I'll do when this trend passes.

I am fortunate it heals. My head heals quickly, relatively speaking, with hardly any sign. My hair even grows back, and these days, with all the shaved heads and tattoos, it wouldn't matter if it didn't. No one notices.

The only thing about it is that as soon as it's healed, I know it can happen again. It's never happened until the previous one is healed, but as soon as it has, I am afraid it will happen again.

•

AN
ENCHANTMENT

· ·

● ●

Why did I put up with it? I almost can't remember, but I make myself: She was The Empress.

She said She was The Empress and that I was a very lucky girl to be among Her chosen.

She showed up out of someplace else and She was covered with the full raiment. She had a helmet with visor. The helmet had a plume and you could see it from afar. The visor covered Her face but there was a slit for Her to see through and the visor could be raised, there were hinges at the jaws and She could raise it up if She wanted and there would be Her face. She had armor all over Her body, a breastplate and shoulder plates and a back plate and thigh and calf plates. She had a magnifi-cent red velvet cape that went from Her shoulders almost to the floor and She was perfectly graceful and fit and big and She looked amazing, She looked like Superman. Her shoulder plates were completely covered with ribbons and medals and decals, the signs of Her marvelous accomplishments and general greatness, a sort of wearing one's resume on one's sleeve. She also had a lot of neck-

●

laces or chains, gold or whatever, around Her neck, some with pendants or signs, and several mysterious, large, tassel-like or peltlike things on Her belt. There was chain mail under Her torso plates. And She had armor boots, pointy as cowboy boots, but very sharp, and with spurs and they were metal and they shone. She was extremely clean and extremely rich, She had to be. She was wearing kid-leather gloves, but they weren't fussy, they were sturdy, beautiful, strong, and there were gold and silver rings and bracelets on the outside and metal plates or whatever on the backs of the gloves, and She had armor on Her fore-arms and arms, but underneath, I could see, I thought, the ends of sleeves made of some exquisite material, buttoned or gathered at the cuffs, and I imagined this exquisite material next to Her skin, right next to Her, and touch-ing Her. She was carrying a staff and a sword and a scepter and a power briefcase and a cellular phone. She had a great belt around Her middle, around Her loins, the one with the mysterious tassel- or peltlike things, and it had a buckle with a sign I couldn't quite make out. The belt was locked.

Thus was She covered from head to toe, that is, from helmet to boot, in the full raiment.

So in fact, I couldn't see Her at all. But I knew who She was, She had to be.

I was in my birthday suit.

She found me out of nowhere.

The place I was was desert-bound, a dreadful, poor, pathetic place, She told me, by comparison to Hers. I believed Her. I'd never seen the like of Her, not in the flesh, though I had dreamt of someone similar. I lived

•

where I lived all alone. I worked alone and it was hard; I was trying to make a garden in the desert.

She came up in a boat. There was no river but She brought it. Like a miracle, She said. The river was the best thing for the garden and She said that She would be the same for me so I believed Her.

She told me, Let me in your house.

I told Her it was rough, the floor was earth, the walls were stone, the only lights were candles and the fire.

She told me, Let me in.

I'd never had a visitor. I let Her in. I gave Her what I'd worked to get, the soup and bread and fruit. She asked me things about myself that I had never thought. I heard me tell Her.

She told me, Let me in your bed.

I told Her it was rough, that it was skins I'd skinned from animals.

She told me, Let me in.

It's true I didn't turn away. It's true, I think, I could have then, more easily than later, but I didn't.

She ran Her fingers, the fingers of Her gorgeous kid and metal gloves through my hair. I heard Her say some things I couldn't understand. She took my hair in both Her gloves and raised it to Her face, that is to Her visor, and I couldn't tell if She looked at it or smelled it or if something in Her armor liked the touch of it but it did something to Her. Then She slowly pulled me down to bed, She pulled me firmly but it didn't hurt and there we lay.

I was uncovered and She parted me, She opened me.

•

We did the thing I'd never known although I recognized. We did the thing She said and I believed Her. Yes, yes, everything she did, I told Her, Yes, I told her, Everything.

So when She said that She would take me back with Her, I went there willingly.

She took me to Her castle and we dwelt within. That is, I dwelt within, both day and night, while She both came and went. She went about Her business as She always had, as if She'd never quit or left or brought me back to be with Her. She wanted no one else to know, She wanted me to be her little secret. But I was in Her bed, where, I admit, at first, I was quite happy to remain. I mean, who wouldn't? For a while.

After all, I'd spent my whole life toiling away in a little garden, which, She had pointed out to me, was not exactly a big deal. I'd never been, as She had also said, in a castle or in a fancy bed. Much less with all day to lie around and watch talk shows and eat bonbons. And sometimes She brought me presents, surprises, like ribbons for my hair, or combs made of amber or shell and sweet-smelling oils and unguents and perfumes. I felt rich. Sure I enjoyed it for a while. Who wouldn't?

I was kept in the room where She kept Her bed. The room was huge and grand and glamorous and ornate. The ceiling was the highest I had ever seen, the chandelier, the most magnificent, from Venice. There were magnificent frescoes on the ceiling, though they were so high above me I could hardly make them out. There were fine tapestries on the walls, from the Gobelin workshop, She assured me, with glorious scenes of battles She had fought and won. There was a particularly handsome scene of Her

•

beheading, or something, some long-haired someone. There were, in fact, numerous scenes of, to my mind, terrible dismemberment. But these things, She assured me, were merely part of Her duties as The Empress. There were wonderful Persian carpets on the floor and honorary degree diplomas from Radcliffe, Vassar, Girton College, and other like institutions. All of this was very impressive to me, as it would be to anyone. But it was all the more impressive because not just anyone could see it. For The Empress told me, She whispered this to me, that this room of Hers was a private room. Extremely private. Off limits to all but the most elect, that is, to Her and—me! I was so touched when She told me this! Also so flattered, if the truth be told. As if—because—I was Her special one, Her chosen one, Her own.

She had a helmet with a visor and She was completely covered, but sometimes when we did the thing She would lift the visor up, I heard the slip of the metal, as sharp as a blade, and I knew part of Her was there, Her knowing mouth, and it would open and I could have seen except I couldn't see because She kept Her glove across my eyes and because She only did this in the dark, but it was Her mouth and it was open, I could feel it.

So She kept me in Her glorious, fine, exotic bed. This bed had silk sheets and a feather mattress and down pillows and a canopy with curious tassellike things hanging from it, similar to the curious tassellike things that hung from Her belt. That is, the bed had everything a girl could want and also, frankly, in my opinion, a bunch of stuff a girl couldn't care less about. As well as a bunch of stuff that I had no idea what it was. But it was Hers, I assumed, so

•

I did not presume to ask. She had muttered something once about people asking things that were none of their goddamn business.

I did not remember this; I should have.

I used to love to lie near Her. I loved to lie when we had done the thing and we were lying quietly. Sometimes She lay there quietly, Her fist clutching a handful of my hair. I loved to watch Her in the light, for She permitted me to light the candles when we were done with the thing. In fact She required candles when She slept. I loved to watch Her, that is, I loved to watch the full raiment that covered Her. I loved to think about what was beneath. I loved it when my skin, which had been altered by the thing, was cooling down, I loved the temperature of the air between Her armor and my skin. I loved the light of the candles against Her armor and the bright of the jewels of Her garments, the brilliance of the helmet. I loved Her knowing, miraculous hands—gloves actually, the knowing hands were covered. The gloves were closed in fists, they were adorned with rings and bracelets, they were covered, yet, I felt, kind. The latter moved me.

She always wore the full raiment. She always, always wore it and it always covered Her. She wore it when we did the thing. She told me this was how it was, the raiment made the girl. She told me it was like that here. I said was everybody like Her here? She said they were in kind, but not degree. For She was more, She was the most, She paused, She loved to say the words, I am The Empress.

The words I loved to hear Her say were I was Hers.

● ● ● ● ●

●

Sometimes I'd go out and wander around. She had a very beautiful castle and a very beautiful town, and very beautiful land was around it. At first I thought about doing a garden, but She wouldn't have it. She said it was low to do that here, and She didn't want my hands like that. Not that She knew much about my hands. For all my hands could know of Her was armor. Everybody in Her town and land seemed nice, but of course I didn't know anyone, I didn't speak their foreign tongue, and none of them were worldly as She, so they could not speak mine. I don't know what they knew of me, if I was Hers or they were always nice to everyone. So everyone was very nice, but no one, nothing, could compare to Her. So mostly I just hung around at home, that is, Her castle, and waited for Her.

She said how they adored Her, and though this was wonderful, it also was a burden. She could never just hang out. She always had to be The Empress with the full raiment. She had to work at being humble, that's why She kept me there. I thought how special I was to Her, that She would tell me this. I thought I saw Her visor lift a bit. My heart began to race as If I was about to see Her, but then it lowered. But I believed I heard Her sigh and I believed I knew this meant She longed to tell me.

So the next time She was doing what She did, I asked Her. Her hands, that is, the gloves were moving on my skin, across my naked shoulders, and I took hold of one of them and stopped Her and I said, Why do you always wear the full raiment? What's underneath?

The gloved hand took a clump of my hair and tugged, then stiffened and stopped moving. There was a shudder then a stillness and She got very quiet. Then I thought I

•

97

WHAT KEEPS ME HERE

was able to discern, amid the necklaces, the kerchiefs, and
the plates, a movement of what must have been Her neck,
and then what must have been Her breast, that indicated,
I believed, that She was swallowing. Nervously, I thought.
I did not remember seeing this before. There was another
breath and another swallow and She tightened her belt
and held the lock, She gripped it in a fist, She drew up
Her shoulder plates, but then She lowered them, they
trembled, and She said nothing.

Then I believed, Oh I believed She longed to tell me,
and for me to see and know Her, but because it was not
in the training of an Empress to be seen or done as She
did me, this would take some time. When She turned
away from me I told myself She needed time and I would
wait for Her. Though She didn't tell me anything at all.

This went on awhile, and I became not only more curious but also impatient. So one time, when She was sleeping, that is, when the breastplate and the shoulder plates
were rising and falling evenly, as though with a sleeper's
breathing, I pulled my body close to Her. I pulled my
naked torso and my naked arms and legs and hands as near
to Her as I could get, so the edge of me was almost beside
the edge of Her. I could feel the cool of the armor, I could
see the belt with the lock. I remember the light from the
candles against Her jeweled armor. I leaned up on my
elbow, over Her and I looked down. My face was above
the helmet and I put my face to the bottom of the visor,
where it could open to Her mouth, and I held my breath
and listened. After several moments when I could no
longer hold my breath, I let it out and thought I heard
something: Her breath? So I held my breath again, but I

•

heard nothing. I shifted up on my elbow and I put my eyes above the eye slit in the visor and I looked inside and I pretended I could see Her. It was dark, but how I wanted to! and then I did, I saw Her face, and then I saw Her look at me, Her eyes were open, and so openly and tenderly and lovingly She looked at me.

I lay beside Her closely and my heart beat lovingly.

Was there an arm against a naked arm? A thigh beside a thigh? Was there a tongue against a neck? A hand, another hand, inside? Was there an opening, a going in, a mouth? Was there a scent, and something wet? Was there desire? Was there the pressing and the kneading, Was there the opening? Was there a word? Were there the teeth and tongue? Was there the longing, light and dark? Was there a flex and a release? Was there the holding and the clutch, and did she open, did she want, Did she desire me?

When I opened my eyes we lay there still, exactly as we were, it seemed, unmoved. Her visor was closed, Her cape and plates were closed, the belt was locked.

But I wondered.

So I asked Her again, a second time. She was lying next to me, and She was doing what She did, and I stopped the movements of Her hands, Her gloves, and said, What covers you—

She pulled Herself on top of me. She pushed my shoulders down and I heard the slip of metal, sharp as a blade, Her visor lifted up and She stuck Her eager, open mouth on mine, I felt Her hungry mouth, it was the only part of Her. She stopped me with a kiss.

A kiss can stop me every time; I learned this terrible thing from her.

● ● ● ● ●

●

I felt a thing within the bed. I picked it up. It was a jewel. It was very red and clear, a ruby. But when I looked at it carefully in the light I could see it was plastic, costume jewelry. There was dried glue on the back. It had been stuck to her armor with schoolroom glue.

The Empress was asleep. Very, very quietly, I slipped down the sheet that covered Her until I found the place where the glass had come unstuck. There was a hole in the surface of Her armor. In the hole were crusty flakes of glue. The work had been done hastily and cheap.

I was lying next to Her and She looked beautiful. That is, the raiment did. I wanted to see Her. I leaned up on my elbow and my hair fell across her armor and shone. I must admit, they looked quite nice together. The helmet with the visor shone like silver in the light, except it wasn't silver, it couldn't have been, not solid anyway, that would have bent. The cape—velour?—was reddish and the fingers of the leather, metal-covered gloves were limp. And then, although they were covered with gold- and silver-colored rings and set with red and blue-green apparently precious stones, I put my naked hand to them. They didn't flinch or move and so I moved my hand toward them and I touched them. I touched the palms of the gloves of the slightly unclosed fists to feel their warmth: I couldn't feel this. I touched the tips of my fingers on the ends of Her buttoned sleeves. I slipped my naked finger up the inside of Her sleeve. I thought I felt a tightening. I slipped my finger further in, I wanted to feel beyond the glove, I wanted to find the skin. I slipped my finger in as far as I could. I could not reach Her.

* * * * *

•

Was this a dream or did I see it when She slept? I open Her visor and drop something in—a penny, a key, a ruby that's real. I hear it fall and it clangs like it is falling through something hollow.

Then a third time I tried to ask Her. We were standing up, we were eye to eye, almost, though I was shorter and She had Her visor on so I couldn't see Her eyes. And I said to Her, What's underneath your raiment?

She looked up. That is, the helmet seemed to look, as if toward the heavens, and it sounded like Her eyelids started to open and close very quickly and Her lower lip began to tremble, or so I imagined because of the movement of Her necklaces, and I was so touched! I thought, She's about to cry! For me! My heart began to swell.

She took a step toward me, I could hear Her armor clank, and then She lifted Her hand, Her glove, and put it on my shoulder. The metal was cold but the leather almost felt like skin. She put Her one hand, one glove, on my shoulder like a comrade, I felt like a comrade, the way we stood almost level, almost eye to eye, though She was taller and I couldn't see Her eyes, only Her visor. But I looked up at the eye slit of Her visor, I looked earnestly, and full of heart, to where I thought Her eyes must be. She squeezed my shoulder the way a comrade would and I knew—I knew—She was about to tell me! But then she gathered up my hair in Her other hand and tugged it back and then She flung out Her arm and slapped me. I was stunned. I stood there while She held me back and slapped me and slapped me again. Then She threw me down and covered my eyes with Her terrible glove and I couldn't see but I heard the scrape of metal, of Her visor,

•

and it suddenly sounded terrible, and I felt the metal and slapping gloves and I felt Her rise above me and Her hand was on my throat and there were cuts and blows and fists and slaps and She did the thing.

The next day after She went out, I got up from the bed and went to the door to leave but it was locked. The windows didn't open, and I sat by them and looked out at Her beautiful town and Her beautiful land and waited. When She came in that night I was afraid and I said nothing. Nor did She. She did the thing and it went on like that.

It went on and on like that. I still do not know how it did, or what it was in me that let it happen. She was bigger than me, huge, and She had all that gear, and it was Her house, and Her castle, and Her town and they adored Her, any one of them would have given her teeth to be Her chosen one. But still. I can't believe I let it happen, I don't know how I did. For I became the thing I did, the thing that was done unto me.

It made me what I was.

And somehow, somehow terribly, I accepted it. I couldn't imagine that I could escape so I didn't try. I thought I deserved what was happening because I had gone with Her willingly, I'd asked for it, I'd wanted Her. And I did not know anyone to tell, I would have been ashamed to tell. And who would ever believe me?

I stopped thinking, I stopped everything. At first She didn't notice but when She did, She said I was stupid, sick, pathetic, and when She said it, it was true. I wasn't anything. I wasn't who I'd been before, I had forgotten I had come from somewhere else, or that there even was a

•

somewhere else. I forgot that I had lived and worked alone and tended a garden. I think it could have gone on like that forever, I think I could have done nothing.

It was The Empress who did something. She told me I had to leave. Then—this, truly, is the worst, the most terrible part—I didn't want to leave Her. I couldn't bear the thought of that. I asked, I begged Her to let me stay. She tried to throw me out but I clung to Her. I said pathetic things to Her, I tried to make Her remember when She'd come to me and what She'd said and done and how She'd brought me here and how I'd done the things She asked and never asked for anything. The Empress was furious. She grabbed my hair and yanked it hard. I felt my throat pull flat, I almost couldn't breathe. She stuck Her visor up to my face and said She'd give me one more chance to get it through my stupid brainless head.

She twisted my neck, I could feel my jaw crack and still, still, I tried to talk to Her. I tried, yes, even then, to see inside Her visor. I thought if I could see Her, if She would let me see Her—But what I saw was all I'd ever seen: the hollow black inside of Her.

She yanked my hair again and She unsheathed Her sword and raised it up. She stood above me. Her sword was bearing down toward my head. Only then did I realize what were the curious pelt- or tassellike things She kept on the canopy of her bed and along Her belt: scalps.

Then—this was a miracle—without my knowing what I did, I wrenched myself away from Her. Her sword came down and whacked the skin off the top of my skull.

But She didn't get enough of me to kill me.

I heard Her howl. The howl was huge and fierce and

•

horrible, and it echoed and amplified inside Her hollow helmet, inside the castle's bedroom walls.

Then somehow, though the door to the room and the windows were locked, again, I don't know how, it was a miracle, I got away.

I ran and fell and crawled but I kept going. My head was bleeding and throbbing. I held it with my hand. I knew to stop the blood I should stop moving but I had to get away so I ran and ran and after a while the blood did stop, I took my hand down from my head and it was red but dry, a scab, so I would heal.

I remember running in the dark, it was the night and cold except the air felt how I hadn't felt in months, or years, I couldn't remember how long, it seemed forever. The air was clear and the night was clear and there were stars and the moon above me and I saw the shadow of myself and it resembled me. I ran as far as my body could and then I fell.

I woke up on a pile of leaves. There was a blanket over me. My head hurt and I put up my hand to touch and it was bandaged. I heard voices and saw a campfire. Three people sat around it speaking quietly. When I sat up the leaves beneath me rustled. The circle of three stopped talking and one of them stood and came to me.

How are you feeling now, she asked.

I told her my head was throbbing. It'll hurt for a while, she said, You had a very close call, but you're going to be all right. Do you think you can eat something yet?

As soon as she said it, I felt how hungry I was. Yes, I said, Thank you.

She said she'd bring something over to me but I wanted to sit with them. I stumbled and she helped me walk. My

●

body was sore and weak. While I ate and drank they told me how they'd found me and brought me here and let me rest. They didn't ask me about myself and I was grateful for that. One of them was wearing a scarf; the second was missing an arm; the third one had a wound I couldn't see. All of us were refugees from something.

I stayed with them as I needed to. They gave me a coat and a scarf for my head and they taught me to navigate by the stars and how to forage for food and water. They taught me to know when to rest. We traveled through the woods by night. We didn't know each others' names, we stayed anonymous. We didn't want who we were running from to find us.

Sometimes I'd wake up in the night and hear one of them weeping. Sometimes she would cry alone, but other times another one would comfort her.

One day one of us said that she was ready. That night we ate our final meal together and washed her and anointed her with oil; we gave her the blessing. The next day she left alone for home.

A few days after she had gone, we found a battered girl in a ditch by the road. I wrapped her in my coat and picked her up and carried her back to our camp. I made her a bed and dressed her wounds and sat with her. In her delirium she shouted things, she cried and wept and shivered. I gave her water to drink and held a cool, wet cloth to her forehead. After her fever broke, we fed her broth and bread. We listened to what she wanted to tell and didn't ask about the rest. In a few days she was well enough to travel so we broke camp and set out again.

We traveled furtively, at night. We found our fellow

•

refugees and took them in and cared for them until they could manage alone.

When I was well enough to be on my own, I told them it was time. That night I ate my final meal with them and they washed me and anointed me with oil; they gave me the blessing. The next day I set out alone to find my way back home.

I traveled by myself awhile. I saw the land around my home that I had never seen. I found my way back to the garden I had left. The garden was in ruins. It was not easy to recover and the work I did was hard but it was good and I revived it.

In the early days when I first returned, I often used to fantasize, when I was breaking brittle wood or cracking open earth, that I was seeing The Empress again. I used to fantasize that I was strong and brave and confident, and I caught Her in a moment She was most adored and I unmasked Her and told everyone, her citizen-slaves, the terrible truth about Her. I dreamt that I told everything, and that I ripped her armor open and I showed everyone what was inside it: Nothing. Or I would dream that She was human, with a body, and that I beat and kicked and trampled Her. I used to dream that I tore off Her helmet, slit Her throat, then slit from Her throat to between her legs, and pulled out the yellow guts of Her and flung them to the dogs and they devoured them. I dreamt that I broke into Her castle late at night with my gang of righteous refugees and we ripped Her out of Her armor and melted Her armor down and gave the money to the poor, the slaves, Her blind and foolish citizens. I wanted to burn Her fucking castle to the ground.

But I did not do any of that.

●

106

* * * * *

I would like to say I overcame. That I grew wise and good and knew that what occurred would never, ever, not to me, again.

But that was not the case.

No, that is not the case.

The case is: To this very day, I can still wake terrified of Her. I dream that I am in Her house, and in Her bed, and She is near, and moving, I can hear the scrape of metal, I am terrified.

There also are the weakest nights, when I thrash and toss and wonder If: If I had been more patient . . . or . . . If I had asked a different way . . . or . . . If had just accepted . . .

It shames me still that I can even wonder.

Still, to this day I'm terrified to say or hear Her name. Still, to this day I can't admit the thing. For I became the thing done unto me, became the thing I did. I can't say what She did to me without saying what I did.

Sometimes I hear of wars or sieges or pillages. That is, I hear of the new campaigns of The Empress, or of Someone else as horrible. I know now there are others just as bad as Her, and worse. I learned from my fellow refugees. And I know that people everywhere are battered, beaten, silenced, disappeared. And though I know there is an underground of fighters, I don't join it. I am not a fighter now, not even in my fantasies. I no longer dream of wreaking vengeance on The Empress.

But if somebody passes near this garden, or I find someone on this land who needs to rest or heal, I take her in and give her what I can. I give her broth and a bed and a coat. I let her stay as long as she needs and I don't ask

•

her anything she doesn't want to tell. But if she wants to tell, I am a witness. I have seen bruises and welts and bones that will not heal. If she wants to get it over with, I stay with her and tend to her and try to keep her comfortable until she breathes her last. Then I lay her broken body in the earth.

I have seen bruises and welts and bones, and I have seen them heal. So if she can and wants to stand, I help her lift the weight of her, we hold her body up. And if she can and wants to walk again, I let her lean against me. She puts her arm on mine and I put mine on her, around her shoulders, back and ribs, around the bruises, breaks and welts. And as she stands and tries to walk, then, underneath my hands, I feel her breath pull in, I feel the blood inside her course and move, the skin of her regathers and together, slow and tentative, we walk. We walk together at her pace, until she, slowly, opening away, begins to loose her arm from me. I feel the body pull away, I feel the body healing. She pulls her body back to her. Alone and by herself, she walks.

She knows that she has found the strength, she knows that she can find her way. Then she takes herself home.

•

A RELATIONSHIP

• •

I wake up in the middle of the night. It's quiet and I
don't know what has woken me. Though I am waiting,
ready, when the phone begins to ring. We haven't been
in touch for years, but I know who it is.

I pick up the phone and she's sobbing. I ask her what
has happened and she says she cannot tell. She sobs and
cries then catches her breath. Her voice is a whisper: It's
awful.

I rush to the house where I know she lives. I try to get in
but the door is locked. I bang on the door. The lights
come on in the upstairs room, then some of the neighbors' lights. I bang on the door and shout and yell until
the downstairs lights come on, the lights in the entrance
hall, the porch.

Then the door I'm banging on is opened and she's in
her robe, the belt is loose, she tightens it and I can see her
skin and she is blinking, sleepy-eyed. She doesn't look like
someone who has just now called me desperately for help.
She rubs her eyes like she has just been woken up. I start
to ask what's wrong, about her call, but then her husband

•

is beside her and she slips her arm around his waist—he's in his underwear—and yawns and makes her darling, sleepy, morning sound. Her husband glares at me.

I take a deep breath and count to ten. Her husband sighs at me like I'm a juvenile delinquent he has caught red-handed doing something stupid. He says, his voice is chilly: Do you have any idea what time it is?

I don't.

She nuzzles her face in the side of his neck and rubs her hand across his washboard stomach.

He keeps his eyes on me.

I start to say something about her call, but when I open my mouth she gives me that pleading old look of hers, the one that begs me not to tell: I don't.

She yawns again and stretches. Her robe rides up, it shows her thighs. She makes her adorable morning sound again, then smiles. First at him and then, a significant moment later, at me.

Then she says, as innocent-sounding as she can, Does anyone want coffee?

My jaw drops open.

Her husband has kept his eyes on me like I'm about to steal the silver. He clears his throat. I don't wait for him to do it twice. I step off the porch and walk down the walk through the tidy lawn, I go through the open gate. When I'm out of the yard I hear him close the door to the house behind me.

Then he locks it.

The phone rings in the middle of the night. Before I pick it up, I know who it is. The way I used to know for years. She knew it too. I put it to my ear and she's already talk-

•

ing. I feel her breath beside my ear, her voice is breathy, frightened-sounding.

It's awful, awful, she sobs.

I'm coming over—

Don't—

I can meet you somewhere.

It's awful, awful, she says again.

We can—

She interrupts, It's *horrible!* It's, It's—Then she is crying, sobbing, speechless.

I run to the house he owns again. Again I bang on the door and shout. The lights in the house come on again, and again in the neighbors' houses. This time some of the neighbors come out to watch. I'm glad because I want this to be witnessed. Again the door I'm banging on is opened and she's standing there. Her robe is partly open and her lips are red, her mouth is almost open, almost begging, I remember, and I grab her arm to pull her away.

But then her husband is beside her, in his underwear, again. He grabs her other arm to pull her back. She stands between us, arms outstretched. Her robe is loose, her breath is fast. I can't tell if she's scared or if—and I hate myself for thinking this, for wondering this again—if she's enjoying this.

I drop her hand. Her husband pulls her in the house. He's got one arm around her and the other on the door that he's about to close to me. He says, his voice is chilly, calm: If you ever set foot in this house again—

I interrupt: She called, she wants me to rescue her— She looks at me with her begging look, to beg me not to tell what she has done. Again, I don't.

I step off the porch and walk through the lawn. I go

●

out through the open gate. Again I hear her husband shut the door to the house behind me.

Lock it.

I don't hear a word from her for ages. I don't call because I have been told I shouldn't, but I can't stop worrying, the way I always have, but more, of course, about her. Then, just when I have almost stopped obsessing, she calls again.

It's late and I am deep asleep. I fumble for the phone, and when I pick it up it crackles like she's very far away. She doesn't tell me who she is the way she did for years. She starts right in: It's awful—

I sit up in bed and look at the clock. It's 2:00 A.M.

It's awful, awful—

What is.

She pauses. I hear her take a deep breath, slowly. Then she says, You know.

I listen to her breathing. I can almost see the way her chest and neck are pulsing. I can almost see her mouth. She doesn't speak while I imagine this. She knows the way I think. And then, when it will be the most effective, she says to me, the way she used to get me most, Oh darling, darling, *please*.

Again, I go to her.

I go to her and go to her because she calls and calls. She calls when he's not there. "To talk," she says, but won't ask me to come to her, then hangs up when she hears him at the door. Then other times, she calls me when he's there and sobs. I go to her then, but when I'm there she acts as if she didn't call. She acts surprised, a bit put out. I know she acts this way for him. I know the way she acts. When

•

he is there, she gives me her look that tells me not to tell about her calls, and so, for her, I don't. Her husband glares and hisses, Don't come back again or else—and hints some vile, veiled threat. But every time I go again, and every time he doesn't do a thing that's different. I think he likes to have me near, the awful past that he can keep reminding her he saved her from.

One time he says he'll call the cops. I tell him, Call! Because I know he won't. I know what he's afraid they will discover.

But even when he isn't there, she never says exactly what the awful thing is I'm to help her from. Perhaps she doesn't tell because she wants me to imagine it. I know she knows I'll think the worst.

Instead when I am there with her, she smiles her pretty smile and shrugs demurely, tells me things are fine. I watch her and I wonder what she hides beneath her blush. She says how sweet of me to stay in touch, and sometime when she has the time, she doesn't now of course, we must have coffee. Then looks around to check her husband hasn't snuck back home. And when she has determined this, she winks at me and whispers, just you and me alone.

I do and I do not, and too, I want and I do not want to believe her. For what she says, or almost says, I think, is truly awful. And one would not want this thing to occur to anyone. But when I try to help her leave, or say she could or should, she answers nothing. That is, sometimes it seems as if she doesn't want escape.

She tells one version once, but then a different one. Then when I ask her, she denies the first. She says I didn't hear her

•

right, deliberately misunderstand. So, quietly, inside myself, I
listen for the changes in her stories. (As I have done with her
before.) I note her hesitations, inconsistencies, denials.

If I'm convinced I know the truth of her, as I believe I
do, what I don't know is why I stay. Why I persist. I don't
know what I think of her—of me, of this. I didn't believe
her once, and then I knew. But it wasn't enough for me to
know; I wouldn't do the leaving. Did I stay to catch her
in the act, to prove her lie to her? And if I did, for what?
To chasten her, to hear her beg forgiveness I would never
give? I don't know why I stayed. Or stay. I know I don't
believe her.

She says I'm awful if I don't believe. She says if I do not,
who will? I think, Exactly. She says that I should know her
more. I do.

I do not want and I want to believe. For I confess
sometimes—I hate myself for this—I hope the awful
things she tells are true. In order that she'd understand, in
contrast, just how decent, and how reasonable, how safe I
was.

I tell myself that when she's understood, she will return
to me. I tell myself that this is what I want, that this is
right. Although I know it's not.

I hate myself for thinking this. I hate what I imagine we
deserve.

I try to not pick up the phone. I want for her to understand how much she needs me. But I wonder, too, if I'm
deserting her, and therefore awful as she says. Or if at last
I am becoming smart enough to extricate myself from just
another, but thank god the last, of her self-serving, silly,
homegrown melodramas.

•

I try to not pick up the phone. But every night I stare at it like someone else is willing it to ring.

The phone rings in the middle of the night. I grab it and before anyone can say anything, I shout, Why do you keep calling me!

There is a gasp.

Do you really want out or not?

No answer.

What do you want me to do?! I shout.

There's a catch in a voice, a muffled sound. Is it the sound of crying? Or another sound, behind it. Something struck? Or someone else? A sob? A blow? A fall?

The phone goes dead.

• • • • •

I wake up in the middle of the night. It's quiet and I don't know what has woken me. Then I hear the banging on the door. Though we haven't been in touch for years, I know it's her.

I slip out of bed and into my robe. I do it very quietly so as to not disturb my sleeping husband. I slip down the stairs and turn on the lights and open the door.

I can't believe she's come to me, as I've imagined, I've desired many times, repeatedly. I planned this scene inside my head for years. Can I pretend to be surprised?

I start to ask her why she's here. I long to hear her say it. But something in my voice is caught. I gasp. It sounds like sobbing. Then she is sobbing too, and she, like me, can't speak, and there is only sobbing, crying, catching breath. I tighten my robe around me.

Then my husband is around me. I feel his body stiffen

•

and slip my arm around his waist to stop him. I want them both to stop, and me. I don't know what to do with what I wanted, got. I need to pull away but I don't know from what. So I pretend, as I have learned, I'm sleepy. I yawn to try to cover what I do not know to say.

My husband sighs. I hope he is relieved that it is her and not a thief. Though, actually, he might prefer a crook so he could have it out, and know exactly who and what it is that he has saved me from.

I put my mouth beside his ear and whisper something he will like. He stares at her then asks, I hear him try to say it calm and chilly: Do you have any idea what time it is?

She doesn't.

I kiss his neck and pat his stomach, mumble "thank you" to him for his tolerance. It's 3 A.M.

She stares at him and he at her and I at each of them. She looks at me and I'm afraid. I recognize that look. She mutters something I can't understand. I wonder if she's threatening. I shake my head to beg her not to say, and she says nothing.

I hug my robe against myself, afraid of what the two of them could do. I stretch my arms and yawn again. Each of them is standing still, unmoving. I smile at them both, at each, and casually as anybody could, I ask, Does anyone want coffee?

She drops her jaw.

I feel my husband. He's breathing fast. I touch his arm to stop him and he stiffens under me. I'm trembling but I keep my hand against him, hope. After a horrible moment of this, he clears his throat.

She gives me another look I recognize, then she jumps off the porch and runs through the yard and out the open

•

gate. My husband watches her every move, he watches her like an animal. When she is out of hearing, he exhales loudly. Then, wordlessly, he takes me back inside the house. He closes the door behind me.

Then he locks it.

I don't say anything about her and my husband doesn't ask. I'm glad. I don't know what I'd say. But also I wish he would because I know he's thinking something but I don't want to bring it up because he will say it only proves how much I think of her.

As if he doesn't.

I stay up after my husband sleeps. I toss and turn away from him then make myself turn back but turn away again, again. This feels the way it did before, familiar. I couldn't stay unmoving where I was. I couldn't stay.

I think about that other place, and someone else I was. I want and I don't want to leave. I want and I do not want to return. I want and I regret that I remember.

I'm here again and doing what I said I wouldn't do. Again. But not again. No, not again.

It's late, and it's occurred again, and I am tender, shamed, to blame, again. And I begin to wonder if, somewhere inside where I don't know, I wonder if I want it.

I pull myself away from him. I have to do so gingerly because of what we've done. This is, there is, a tenderness that's unlike any other.

I slip away to another room. I sit in the dark and try to remember, imagine, what was before. She warned me, but

●

in anger, that it would not be the same, it would be worse. But I would not believe her then. I don't know how this differs from the other place I left.

I don't remember when the promise broke.

Again, I do not stop myself. I call her.

She answers the phone immediately. She's waiting for my call the way she used to. How I used to too. I know she knows it's me and I regret that I have called. I want to tell her nothing, not about this house, or him, or how she hovers in between us. And I'm afraid she'll ask and I will not know how to tell what keeps me here.

My voice sounds strange when I start to speak. I want to lie but fear that even lying, she will know me.

I say what I don't want to her. Then she prevaricates, we interrupt and second-guess and lie.

Perhaps she tries to offer or explain or compromise, but I don't want to hear again, or say again, our tired, worn-out reasons, explanations, our excuses.

I don't know how we end this conversation. I do know that we do not say good-bye.

I stand behind the door and wait. I know she'll come, despite what I have said. She knows which part of what I say I mean. I press myself against the door. I feel the hard and cool against my flesh. I look out through the hole for her. The night is dark, the streets are dim. I know the way she'll walk to here.

I used to live there once.

I told her once, when being somewhere else was not conceivable, and when whatever I would tell her she would tell me, Yes, I told her I would never, no, that it

•

would be impossible, the worst, and I would rather die, and if it ever happened she must rescue me, or help, or put me out of misery, or murder me, but somehow get me out. I told her then, no matter what I told her, if it happened it would be a lie and only said beneath duress. I told her to remember that and promise she would do what I was begging now.

But now I am afraid because I know how she remembers. I do not mean what I said then, and I can't make her see that I have changed. No, truly, changed. Though also sometimes, I admit I doubt. I don't know if I have.

I stand behind the door and wait. I watch her through the hole. I see her hand approach the door, then both her striking fists and I remember. Her face is splotched with white and pink. She's frantic, longing, breathing hard. Her mouth is open, crying out. She looks like she's in pain, almost. Her skin is tight, her breasts and shoulders heave, there is the spring of sweat across her neck. She bangs her fists, her body up against the door. I press myself against it and it shudders. I hold my body there and it remembers.

She hits and cries but can't get in.

I want to keep myself from her but don't want her to leave.

I turn on the lights and act like I have just come down the stairs. I open the door and see, familiarly, her fists are raised. I move my finger to my lips to tell her, Quiet.

Perhaps she thinks that I'm about to strike. She flings an arm up, grabs my hand. I want to say it wasn't how it looked, but I know not to use that line again.

And then my husband is behind me, and he grabs my other hand and pulls me back toward the house. The wind

•

is knocked away from me. I don't know if it's him or her who did it. I feel my other hand in hers. She's gripping tight and so is he. She's strong as I remember. So is he. And I am in between them and they're pulling.

I gasp, she drops my hand, my husband pulls me. He's got one arm around me and the other on the door that he's about to close. He pushes me inside the house. He partly shuts the door then leans outside and hisses something I can't understand.

I think I hear her shouting something back.

I feel him pull away, and I'm afraid what he would do, or she, or they, if he went out to her. I pull him in the house with me. He slams the door. She jumps off the porch and runs through the yard. I close my eyes and almost see her running down the street, to home. I almost feel the touch of the air against her skin, the tightening and firmness of her thighs. I almost see the rising and the falling of her breast, I almost hear her heavy breathing—

What I hear is my husband lock the door behind me.

● ● ● ● ●

I wake up in the middle of the night. It's quiet and I don't know what has woken me. A nightmare? Dream? But maybe I didn't sleep at all. Not after what she said. Not after what I said and did again. I don't know how we got to bed, what lies or threats we used. I don't know how we came to this.

I wish she would forget, I wish that I had never known, I wish she hadn't done—She says it's over, done. I don't believe her. I know the way she thinks and acts. I've seen in her what she has not.

I turn in bed toward her but she isn't there. I sit up,

●

half-asleep and hear, I think, though I am not sure of the order: a knocking, a banging on the door. A desperate, hissing whisper. Is it the phone? Or at the door? Is it the rustle of her robe as she is running down the stairs? I turn on the light and look at shape her body pressed in bed. It looks like she is turned from me. I stumble out of bed— I'm in my shorts—and run to find her.

The lights downstairs are on. My wife stands in the open door. Her robe is loose, I see her back, she's leaning out, away from me. I hear her saying something, but perhaps it's someone else who talks. I can't hear if it's speaking, crying, sobbing. I step behind her and see who she is talking to. She slips her arm around my waist to prevent my doing what I might. This time she does. The person who is there is her: my wife's old lover.

I can't believe she's here where she knows she's not allowed. My wife and I agreed to this. She said they hadn't been in touch for years. This confirms how right I was to not believe her. I can't believe she's here just now, exactly when my wife and I have quarreled.

I take breath in deep and count to ten. My wife leans into me and whispers something sweet to try to calm me. I don't know why she still wants to protect her.

I stare at her. In the porch light she looks shadier, more thin than I remember. I bet she's gone downhill more quickly since she's been without my wife.

She always was the worst for her. She made my wife— she was—together—they were—worse, hysterical. My wife has told me many times that it was awful, horrible: She was. My wife would have suffered unspeakably had I not found her then. It's me she has to thank for her recovery. Unlike her ex, I am responsible.

•

I hate the very thought of her. The sight of her can physically repulse me. I take a deep breath, count to ten again. I try to feel pity, the way I'm sure my wife did: She's a mess. I say to her, the ex, as if she's a delinquent I am losing patience with: Do you have any idea what time it is?

She stares at me, a hoodlum, but she doesn't speak.

My wife nuzzles the side of my neck and rubs her hand across my stomach. She's trying to make me look at her, to look away from her awful ex. I don't. I stare at her.

She starts to make some rank excuse, then stops herself. She knows she can't charm me the way she did my troubled wife.

My wife puts her hand above her mouth and closes her eyes and yawns. This makes her look, as it always does, so vulnerable. I pull my arm around her tight. She stretches her arms above her head and yawns again the darling way she does in bed each morning. She says to me, Do you want coffee?

The ex stays on the porch in front of us like the irritating bore who always is the last to leave the party. I look at her and clear my throat.

She stumbles off the porch. I wonder if she's drunk—I know she shared this problem with my wife. She stumbles through the yard and out the gate. My wife and I go back inside the house.

I close the door behind us and she slips away from me. She hurries down the hall and to the kitchen. I'd thought she wasn't being serious about the coffee—it must be 3 A.M. I follow her to the kitchen, where she's already grinding the beans.

Are you really making coffee, I ask. I have to raise my voice above the grinder.

•

When she finishes grinding, she answers brightly, Sure! and gets out a filter.

It's 3 A.M., I say. Aren't we going back to bed?

I'm awake, she says, I think I'll just stay up awhile. She smiles her sweetest smile at me then reaches up into the cupboard. Her robe rides up and I see the back of her thighs. They're white and tight, with spots of faint, faint blue. They look like they belong on an older woman. She gets out her favorite coffee cup; she doesn't get out mine.

You're not making any for me?

You didn't sound like you wanted any, she says. She doesn't turn to face me.

I want to go back to bed.

I'll be up in a while.

I know to not believe her. I take her shoulders and turn her around to face me. What was that all about, I ask.

She squints out the window as if there's something to see. Oh, I don't know . . .

She's stalking you, I say.

Oh, come on—

She found out where you live.

She pulls her body away from me and turns on the faucet. How did she find out where we moved?

She shrugs. Fills the carafe with just enough water for one.

Has she been in touch with you?

She puts the carafe in the coffee machine. She doesn't answer me.

Did you—

She spins around and shouts, No! Then catches herself.

Honey, she says, That was years ago—

I told you I didn't want her here.

•

She folds the edge of the coffee filter.

You don't know what she did to you.

She measures the coffee. Her elbow shakes.

Maybe you've forgotten what that woman did to you.

My wife spins around and snaps at me: I haven't forgotten the things she did. Again and again you remind me—

She says it like a threat, which is unlike her. She spins back around to the coffee machine and shoves the filter in. My wife has turned her back to me. I watch her shoulders rise and fall and hear her breathing heavily.

I need to show her that it's different. I grasp her shoulder with my hand. She flinches, gasps. I look at the back of her head and say, my voice is calm, There's nothing to be afraid of.

My wife does not turn back to me. She continues to face the coffee machine. I feel her shoulder shake. I take a deep breath. My wife neither moves nor speaks. I count to ten. The machine begins to gurgle. My wife's shoulders are still, then rise, as she takes one deep breath, then fall. She tightens her belt around her robe. Then I feel her move her arm and hear her click the coffee off. Then she turns around to face me.

She smiles agreeably and says, Okay, I'll come to bed.

I step aside for her to pass. She leaves the kitchen and goes up the stairs. I turn out the light and go up the stairs behind her.

●　●　●　●　●

It isn't me, it isn't me. They try to make me take the blame, I won't. I'm not a monster. No. I'm not the monster.

●

126

It isn't me, it's them: It's *her*. Why don't I tell her this right out?

They don't admit the things they do. I do. That is, I do in reason. What's private here is no one else's business. People misinterpret, think the worst. I wish they had, the two of them, some decency, discretion. I wish I could have—

I am not the one who's sick.

Although I loathe myself for staying here, I don't know why I do.

I tell myself I will this time, this time will be the one. Or be the last. That I will prove and they will see. But who am I trying to show it to? Or prove?

It isn't good for me, or right. But I put up with it. It isn't good for her.

But maybe it is. Maybe it's the only chance, therefore my duty.

I don't know what I'm fighting with—against. I cannot tell what keeps me where I am.

If I could get—If I could have—If I—I don't know what I'd do that would be different.

I say I can't abide, that it is awful, but I stay. I could walk out, I think, away and not look back, except I long to look and have the right. I want to see and demonstrate. Though I'd be better blind, I am, if I could not look back or see, and not remember.

I don't know if I could, but I believe, I think, I must, that I desire not to, for I don't. I think, because I must, because I couldn't bear it otherwise, it isn't me, it's one of them, it's someone else that keeps coming back and staying here unmoving where I am, that keeps me here.

•

WHAT KEEPS ME HERE

. . . .

•   •

The two are held together by the one. Each is about four inches wide, two inches thick and very long. They never have been warped or bent. I think they must have grown with me, although I don't remember being less or different. They always fit as they have always been.

The belt that holds them goes around. I've counted two loops, perhaps three, but I forget. I should not have, in the first place, been so curious. I should not have touched it but I have. I felt it hard to learn the texture, size, and shape of it, and if there is a way that I could slip away but there is not, and how many times around. The belt is about three inches wide, possibly a holdover from the sixties, that embarrassing, if not actually dangerous, decade for fashion. The belt is buckled with a buckle. I have felt the buckle too. It is cool, metal, with a slightly burnished texture and a relief design. Perhaps it is one of those bronze belt buckles, also from the sixties, with perhaps an astrological, western, or military motif. I believe I could read the relief of the buckle if it were a word like *Peace* or *Love* or even a peace sign, but it is not: I don't know what it says. Of course I have never seen it.

•

I have felt with my hands for any belt holes with which the belt might be adjusted. Tighter or—oh if only!—looser.

I have also felt the metal catch that goes through the hole that keeps the belt so tight around my head. There is no give.

The belt covers my eyes. The two boards cover and nearly flatten my ears. I bet I look like some ridiculous cartoon character, a stupid hapless goof being punished for having said some unkind thing about some dopey, donkey-eared kid at school. Although I cannot for the life of me remember what I said, what I ever even could have said, to deserve this. I tried very hard to be nice, and I believe I was. But I must have done something, I had to have, and it must have been something wicked, something terrible. For this can't be the way it simply is. I must be being given what I'm due. There must be some right reason.

It is absolutely dark, I can't see anything.

The bottoms of the boards press into my shoulders where my shoulders go into my neck. I feel the bottom of the boards all the time like I am growing against them and they don't give. That is, only enough to keep me.

I'm wearing a little cotton undershirt with skinny little straps. It's all I have.

I used to try to twist away but I no longer try. Not only did it hurt like hell, it also, more important, was wrong. It was not right, it is not right.

But back then, when I tried, I did so carefully. I said out loud, and that was not just whistling Dixie, I assure you, because even the tiniest movement of my throat or jaws or tongue hurt like hell. It hurt to try to speak, but I said out loud, although I do not know to whom, so soothingly,

•

respectfully, like a smooth-skinned little girl to a frothing dog, "I'm going to lift my hands, okay? That's all. Okay?" then lifted my arms as slowly as I could, as if my being slow would keep the dog from lunging. But I couldn't move the slightest bit without the muscle and the skin across my shoulder moving and getting torn. But I was valiant. I had the patience of a saint, although it feels not quite comfortable to make this comparison. I gritted my teeth and lifted my empty hands to the belt and felt. I tried to loosen the belt but it would not loosen. Rather, tightened, and hurt like hell. I took my hands away and lay them in my lap and said, although I do not know to whom, "This can't—this can't be how it is."

Another time I raised my hands and slid my hands up the length of the board to feel the top. I reached as high as I could reach but I could reach no top. There was no end. The boards went on forever and they pressed on me from somewhere up where I could never reach: where is what put, what keeps me here.

Sometimes, to pass the time, I tell myself I see something. I tell myself sometimes I see a light.

Sometimes no matter what I know I hope.

I'm sitting in a straight-backed wooden chair.

I have felt the wood of the chair with my hands. I have lowered my hands slowly and carefully and run my fingertips around the sides of the chair and gripped the sides. I have moved my hands in only a very small shape but I have moved them thoroughly through that. I have done everything I could, I think.

●

I think the grain of the wood of the chair I'm in is the same as the grain of the wood of the boards.

I don't know how I got here.

The belt extends up slightly above my eyebrows and down to slightly below the bones of my eye sockets. That is, to just below my cheekbones. It is a thick belt. Yes, it must be from the sixties. But I was just a child then, a little girl, I wasn't even a teenager then. I was not a rebellious youth.

I didn't ask for this.

I have tried to lift myself but something keeps me down. I have tried to slip away but I am kept.

Sometimes I feel a breeze against the back of my neck. That's nice. Sometimes I am so tired and start to drift and my head starts to drop and the boards jut into my collarbone. That perks me up. I right myself and clench my fists and sit up straight again. (The one correct position is the upright one.) I am to keep my hands still on my lap, my head straight ahead and both eyes closed. As if I could see anything. I am not to open them.

Except I do.

Sometimes—perhaps it's seasonal, like asphalt in the winter or like windowsills that will not budge in high humidity. Or maybe on a schedule that I do not understand. Or maybe in response to something I've been thinking, I hope, I'd love—

I've tried to note a pattern but I can't. Perhaps it's only on a whim. In any event, sometimes—oh sometimes sweet!—it loosens.

●

I live for these times. Each time I tell myself one time—

Though in those times, sometimes, although I know that I should not, because I can because the belt is not so tight, though I am not permitted to, I look.

I open my eyes beneath the belt and in the sliver of light between the belt and the skin of the edge of my nose—oh god.

There are dangers. One time, though maybe more than once, I always am confused between what happened and what never did, but one time, once, I think, I opened my eyes and looked and it was black, the same as when my eyes were closed, but it felt different. The different feeling was something. But then when I needed to blink, my eyelid—the left? the right? I can't remember—wouldn't close. Whether it got caught against some moisture or some thing inside the belt, though whatever else could get inside the belt, there isn't room for anything, there's hardly room for me, or only somehow folded itself against itself, I couldn't close it. I opened both eyes wider as if I could unstick the one. Then—this shows how foolish I was—I lifted my hand—was it my left? or right?—and put my fingers on the belt above the place as if I could touch my bad eye through the belt. The boards dug in my shoulders and I hurt like hell. It happened in an instant. I only acted on instinct. I am not to blame.

The skin of my shoulders tore and it was sharp. The press against my head was awful. And my poor eye—the left? or right?—remained half open, bent and stung. I lowered my hand to make the pressure on my shoulders less. It was a while before I felt less. It was a long, long time my eye stung terribly.

•

Then after a long, long time, by itself, and not resultant from a thing I did, the eye was closed.

The way how was a mystery to me.

I was so grateful for the closing and I promised, though I do not know to whom, that never would I ever, ever, ever attempt to open my eyes again. That thus I would remain forever, humbled.

But I'm not good at promises.

I've made them that I haven't meant, though at the time I did, I thought, though really only made them as a bargain, begging I might get I away or through the thing I cannot bear.

It was not only wickedness that made me break my promise.

Because of the bridge of my nose there are two tiny little slivers of space where the belt does not press always entirely flat. Through which, sometimes, if I open my eyes and roll them down, I can, some rare times, see.

And what I see sometimes is not the dark. But sometimes what I think I see is light. And I believe, no matter what I know, there is a light and I believe that I will see it some. And I believe that this will not endure forever, no, though for the time foreseeable. But I believe that there will come a time when belt and boards will be undone, will loosen, and what holds me down, what keeps me here, will fall away, and I believe that I will rise, yes, I believe that I will see.

•